YESTERDAY
Never, *Ever* Dies

SIMON TRICK

Grosvenor House
Publishing Limited

The right of Simon Trick to be identified as the author of this
work has been asserted in accordance with Section 78
of the Copyright, Designs and Patents Act 1988

The book cover picture is copyright to Simon Trick

This book is published by
Grosvenor House Publishing Ltd
Link House
140 The Broadway, Tolworth, Surrey, Kt6 7Ht.
www.grosvenorhousepublishing.co.uk

A CIP record for this book
is available from the British Library

ISBN 978-1-78623-806-1

To my dear wife, Nazy, who constantly
supports me in all my endeavours.

To Ileesha Singh,
for inspiring the writing of this book,
being a great audience and a helpful critic.

SATURDAY

~❦~

Sunlight streamed through the partially open, deep pink curtains into Rebecca's eyes.

"Mmm...go 'way, Mum," she murmured. "Wanna sleep..."

"Not today you don't! Come on, get up and have a shower, or you'll be having a bad hair day." Rebecca Roberts rolled on to her side and pulled the duvet over her head. A mischievous grin spread slowly across Sarah Roberts' face. "You're as bad as your Dad," she said, casually. "He can't drag himself out of bed without my help, either. Now," a sinister note crept into her voice, "where's that ice-cold, wet sponge I used on him earlier..."

"What?" Rebecca sat bolt upright in her bed.

"Didn't you hear that yell just now?" her mother's voice was sweetness; but the mischievous grin had become a smile of pure evil. "Ohh...here it is..." A dripping, lumpy, butterscotch object emerged from behind her mother's back, lovingly cradled in her left hand. Rebecca's eyes widened in horror.

"I'm up! I'm up!" she yelled, leaping from her bed, through the bedroom door and into the shower at high speed.

"Works every time," said her mum, under her breath.

Rebecca was a tall thirteen-year-old, with a slim, athletic physique. Her short, raven hair and green eyes made her a distinctive figure in her school. Normally, a warm, welcoming person, she nevertheless grimly considered the day ahead, while towelling her hair dry. A summer barbecue with her relatives! Uncle Gary and Aunt Leanne would be coming with their children; and they were always bad news.

Jamie was five and trouble. Rebecca couldn't prove it, but the delight on his face at the breakfast table when she stormed in with a face like thunder was enough to tell her – he was the one who left worms in her bed!

The girls were no better, she thought. Emily at seven was annoyingly ingratiating. She was always flattering Rebecca on how pretty she looked in her jeans, dress, skirt, T-shirt...yet it sounded hollow and unconvincing, as if she was being nice because she wanted something from her. And things went missing from Rebecca's bedroom after every visit – usually something Emily had taken a shine to – but again, nothing she could prove.

Jasmine, meanwhile, was Rebecca's age. Their hair was the same colour and their eyes were almost the same shape; but where Rebecca was tall and slim, Jasmine was shorter and stockier. Rebecca often caught resentful looks and half-heard mutterings under Jasmine's breath whenever Uncle Gary compared the two of them and teased Jasmine about her weight. But it wasn't Rebecca's fault after all and she never laughed when Uncle Gary said it. Still, Jasmine kept her distance and Rebecca had given up caring.

As for her Uncle Gary and Aunt Leanne...*the less said*, thought Rebecca, *the better!*

Rebecca closed the door behind her and stepped on to the gravel path surrounding her house. Yellowish-brown Scots Pine needles drifted down onto her pink T-shirt, from twenty metres above her head. Normally, she looked daggers at the giant trees: it was always Rebecca who had to clear bags of the needles off the pathway – did they *ever* stop falling?

This time, though, she brushed them away carelessly. Her attention had been caught by the appearance in the cul-de-sac of a large furniture lorry, which had pulled up outside her home, opposite the house with clusters of pine and fir trees engulfing the building.

She watched as the lorry backed, slowly, into the concrete driveway, then gradually disappeared behind the huge evergreen trees and bushes.

"I wonder who's moving in?" said Rebecca, aloud. "Anyone my age, maybe?"

Wandering across the needle-covered road, pine cones ricocheting off each other as they bounced off her sneakers, Rebecca peeked down the shadowy pathway, trying to get a glimpse of the new residents of 20, Pine Tree Close...

"Rebecca! Where are you?" It was Dad. "We've got to get the house tidy in one hour!! Come on, you're sweeping the path, remember?"

Rebecca's eyes swept up to the skies in despair. Violent thoughts of chainsaws slashing through pine trees, flashed through her mind.

"One day..." she muttered to herself.

"I love your ring! It's beau'ful," crooned Emily over Rebecca's silver ring, which had little red and green stones set in circular patterns.

"Thanks. Dad gave it to me for my birthday."

"Can I try it on? Jus' for a minute!"

"Um…well…" Rebecca prevaricated, nervous of her cousin's light-fingered ways.

"Go on, Becks! Let 'er 'ave it for a mo'! She won't 'arm it!" Uncle Gary laughed, blowing a plume of vape up into the air and winking at Emily.

Rebecca didn't want to start a quarrel, but she didn't trust her. As she passed her the ring, she determined to keep a close eye on Emily, whose eyes widened, greedily.

"One minute ONLY!" hissed Rebecca.

"Yeah, yeah…" Emily replied as she slipped it on to her middle finger and turned away quickly, rushing out of the open patio door and into the garden.

Rebecca started to chase after her when a human missile collided with her and she collapsed on to the lounge floor. Jamie, grinning down at her, sat on her stomach.

"I got some insects! Look!" He held out a hand full of woodlice in to her face. She grimaced inwardly. Rebecca hated creepy-crawlies. But she would not show it: especially not to him!

"They aren't insects, they're crustaceans," said Rebecca, fixing him with her gaze. "Insects have three parts to their body and only six legs. Woodlice have a rigid, long exoskeleton and fourteen legs." Confusion replaced Jamie's grin. "Now we've got that sorted… GET OFF ME!" He scrambled off her, hurriedly.

"No need to speak to your cousin like that! He's only little!" Aunt Leanne waddled over to Jamie and gave him a cuddle. "He's only being friendly, aren't you, darling?" She wiped his nose, which was running as usual. "You should learn manners, young lady!"

Rebecca bit her lip and decided to leave the room immediately – better than another quarrel with her aunt. *How did Dad get a sister like her?* It wasn't just that she was short and blonde and he was tall and dark. *He* always looked for the best in people and was willing to listen to other people's points of view. *She* always picked out people's faults and she was *never* wrong; at least, not in her opinion.

Outside the house, Rebecca charged out of the front gateway, seething. Only the fresh breeze – and the feeling of freedom – helped calm her. A few stones skittered across the road from the gravel path. Absent-mindedly following them, she kicked them again and again, until she found herself back at the tall, black, wrought iron gates of their new neighbours' house.

Rebecca peered through the swirling, upright bars of the gate. Nothing. Not a sight or a sound. They were keeping themselves to themselves. Curiosity gnawed at her, like a mouse attacking a bag of flour. Who were they? Were there any children? Any pets? How many people moved in?

"I must find out. Perhaps I'll have the chance to see, tomorrow," said Rebecca, to herself. "Ah well. Back to the guerrilla war with my cousins!"

SUNDAY

The next morning was a complete contrast to the day before: rain instead of sun, wind instead of calm…and no uncle, aunt or cousins!

Yes!

But what to do? A thought struck her. She hadn't seen Ida – her next-door neighbour – for a few days. Perhaps she needed some shopping and, anyway, Rebecca didn't care about rainy weather.

"Hello, love," Ida's crinkly face lit up in a lovely smile. "Come on in from that rain." She led Rebecca slowly away from the deep blue paint of her front door and down the dark corridor to her living room. "Have a seat, love. Like a cuppa tea?"

"Yes, please, Ida." Rebecca glanced around the room that she had grown to know so well. It hadn't changed since she had first met Ida when she was only a toddler: the brightly patterned black and red carpet; the porcelain cats on the mantelpiece; the faded, family photographs in black and white; some colour ones from the sixties and seventies of her with her husband smiling, happily, out at her; the slightly stuffy but cosy atmosphere that pervaded the room. It was all still the same.

"Would you like a hand to bring the tea in?" called Rebecca.

"No thanks, love. I've got my trolley," replied Ida. Within a minute, she was wheeling in the tea. "Got some of your favourite biscuits too, dearie. And there's two sugars in your tea, as usual."

"Thanks, Ida," smiled Rebecca. "You make the best tea."

"Earl Grey. Me Mum always thought I was a bit posh when I started using it just after I got married, but Shahin loved it an' then I got a taste for it." She stared over at her husband's picture, her eyes misting over. "I still miss 'im, Becca."

Rebecca smiled. Only Ida called her 'Becca'.

"He was very handsome, your Shahin."

"Yeah. Heart of gold, too." Ida paused. "Becca, how come you don't spend more time with people your own age? You shouldn't be spending so much time with an old lady like me."

Rebecca thought for a moment and then her answer rushed out of her in one go.

"I don't know, Ida. The girls round here are into boys, boy bands, make-up and shopping. That's ok, I mean…I like boys and boy bands too, but I want to do other things right now. I love my gymnastics and taekwondo. I put a lot of time into them 'cos I think I'm good at them. Most of the girls I know in school do the same sports that I do. But they don't live anywhere near here. And…even they…well, they see the world in a really narrow way, like…anyone a bit different from them isn't worth knowing and should be avoided. But I don't feel that way about people…wherever they come from it's what makes them interesting. But, as for my cousins! They don't know anything. And Auntie Leanne and Uncle Gary are even worse. They really get on my nerves… But you're not like that, Ida, I can talk to you about anything."

"You know, Becca," said Ida, raising her eyebrows, "You should give your cousins a chance. They might surprise you one day. Not everyone has the same chances in life as you have. And not all parents are as good as your mother and father.

"I reckon I was really lucky. Y'know, when Shahin asked me to marry him, back in the 1950s, I thought my Mum would never go for it, what, with him coming from Iran an' all."

Rebecca looked surprised. "Why should it matter where he came from? I'm friendly with lots of people from lots of other countries. Wasn't that normal, then?"

"Oh no, love," replied Ida, "It was different times, different attitudes. A lot more prejudice in them days. At that time, black people from the Caribbean was coming here looking for jobs. I remember some boarding houses, sort of like Bed and Breakfast places, putting up signs saying 'No dogs. No Blacks'. That's what lots of people felt like – they was scared and nervous of people looking different and dressing different.

"So I thought my Mum would be a bit shirty with Shahin. But I underestimated her. True to say, she was taken aback at first an' a bit suspicious of him, what with his different accent, slightly darker skin…anyway, she always thought I'd go for blond-haired Reggy Harris from down the road, 'cos we'd been friends since we was kids. He ended up running a chain of betting shops! Quite well-off he became: big house, lots of cars. Nice wife he had, too. We still stayed as friends, though. Died last year, poor Reggy and you should 'ave seen his funeral! Horse-drawn glass carriage…the lot!

"But anyway," continued Ida, "when my Mum could see I was determined – always stubborn, me – Mum decided to give Shahin a chance, an' soon she really loved him. Maybe you could do the same for your cousins. I mean, they're only young an' they are family."

Rebecca wasn't convinced, but she said nothing. Ida always gave her something to think about.

"Did you know that a new family has just moved in to the Close, Ida?" said Rebecca, changing the subject. "They've taken over the Jordans' old place."

"Oh, really? What do they look like, then? 'Ow many of them are there?"

"I don't know. The van went behind the trees so I couldn't see anything. But," said Rebecca with a grin, "I'd like to find out."

"'Ere, what've you got in mind, young lady? I know that look!" Ida couldn't stop smiling back at the twinkle in Rebecca's eyes.

Half an hour later, the two friends were making their way towards the large, closed gates, with a couple of packets of chocolate biscuits between them.

"Well, love, we're here." Ida looked steadily at Rebecca. Rebecca grinned back at her, then, taking hold of the gate handle-ring with the ridged pattern, she turned it. Or at least, she tried to turn it. It wouldn't budge. Putting her whole, athletic body behind it, she tried again and this time felt it shift, rustily, in its housing. The gate, juddering heavily and loudly like an antique washing machine, gradually opened.

"Needs oil," remarked Ida, "and weedkiller," she said, eyeing up the pathway. "The Jordans really let things go to the dogs over the last couple of years.

I s'pose they just got too old to look after such a big place. Yeah…I know just how they felt."

Rebecca caught the note of sadness in her voice and stopped in her tracks. "You're not old, Ida!" she said, putting a hand on Ida's arm.

Ida hesitated before she spoke.

"It's like, I still feel and think I'm twenty, but Becca, I look in the mirror every day and it doesn't lie to me about the bags under me eyes and the crinkly skin. I get up in the morning and it gets harder to put one foot in front of another: I ache in me joints and…and…I still miss Shahin!" Her eyes welled up. Rebecca hugged her.

"Maybe this wasn't such a good idea. It's made you sad, coming here to a house where your friends used to live."

Ida gently removed her arms and wiped her eyes with her sleeve.

"No, I'm just being stupid and selfish an' Shahin wouldn't thank me for that. Come on, Becca, let's knock on that door!"

The pathway, lined by huge fir trees, stretched away in a dark, sinister line next to the towering walls of the house. A chill ran up Rebecca's spine. Was it the rain? She wasn't sure. They walked on, arm in arm till they reached the entrance to the house. It was immense. A giant, brick-edged arch surrounded by a white, smooth cladding, with more bricks set in geometric patterns in different parts of the wall. Underneath the archway at the top of four marble steps, stood massive, oak double-doors with small, stained glass windows above door handles that were sisters to the one on the gate. Beside the right-hand door was a long, black rod of metal

– with the same ridged design from the gate – which hung down from the ceiling of the arch. Rebecca looked at it, uncertainly.

"That's the *door-bell*," said Ida, raising an eyebrow at her young companion.

"Oh," replied Rebecca, feeling very stupid.

"Give it a pull, then." Ida nudged her. Rebecca felt in awe of the size of the house. Reluctantly, she reached out and tugged it, gently.

She heard nothing.

"Give it a *proper* pull!"

Rebecca went bright pink and yanked the rod hard!

Distantly, she could hear the resonant tone of a bell, somewhere deep inside the 'mansion'. Rebecca and Ida waited…and waited…and waited. Rebecca began examining her sneakers for dirt, while Ida shuffled from side to side, uncomfortably. How long were they going to take? The wind swirled around the entrance, chilling the air, unseasonably. Rebecca glanced over at Ida, again.

"Maybe we should…"

CLUNK, CLUNK!

The sound of heavy bolts being drawn back stopped her in mid-sentence. The door began to open, very slowly. They raised their gaze until they were staring into two, large, very dark eyes, watching them from behind a narrow gap between the door and its frame. Rebecca shuddered.

"H-h-he-hello," she stuttered.

The eyes continued their appraisal of the two friends. He, or she – they couldn't tell which – said nothing.

"I'm Ida and this is Rebecca. We're your neighbours and we wanted to say hello and welcome you to Pine Tree Close." Ida felt no fear.

"Mmm," came the reply from behind the door: a low, rumbling, like the engine of a massive lorry that made the whole entrance shake – hardly a human voice at all.

"W-w-we b-brought some biscuits for you," Rebecca stammered, holding out the packets.

"Mmmmm."

"Well, p'raps we should just leave the biscuits for you," suggested Ida.

"Mmm."

Ida motioned to Rebecca to place the packets near the doorway. Then they backed off, slowly.

"Well, goodbye!" called out Rebecca, hanging on to Ida's arm. She was shaking, but trying not to show it. The huge arch receded as they carried on their backward trek, until they could no longer see the doorway. Then Rebecca turned quickly and practically dragged Ida to the gate.

"Slow down, love!! I'm no spring chicken! You're killin' me arthritis!"

"S-sorry, Ida," mumbled Rebecca, pushing her into the street and hauling the gate shut. "I-I just felt…"

"…we was in danger?" proposed Ida.

"Mmmm," came the mumbled response.

"Yeah. Wasn't what I'd call a *warm* welcome. Let's go and have another cuppa tea and some cake…they've 'ad all me biscuits!"

"What! You CANNOT be serious!!"

"It's no good shouting, Rebecca! There's no other way…Your Mum and I have already discussed it."

"Don't *I* get a say?"

"Of course you do."

"I say NO!"

"You're outvoted."

"That's not fair!"

"Your cousins are going to be staying here for the next few days."

"But *why*?" Rebecca fumed.

"Because…" her father took a deep breath and ran his hands through his thick, dark hair, "…because your Auntie Leanne has had an accident."

"Oh yes?" Rebecca raised a disbelieving eyebrow. "What *sort* of accident?"

"She…was rushing after Emily and Jamie who were trying to stop the ice-cream van, when she slipped on a…banana skin…"

"Ahrrch!" A noise erupted from Rebecca that was a cross between blowing her nose and a cough. One hand went over her mouth and the other leant against the kitchen breakfast bar, as she tried not to laugh. A grin played, edgily, at the corners of her father's mouth. Even *he* had to admit that the thought of his sister doing a comedy slip on a banana skin while running for an ice-cream was hilarious.

"…and…she landed…on her coccyx!"

"Mmmha-ha-hmmm!" Rebecca doubled up and stuffed a tea towel into her mouth.

"REBECCA!" Terry Roberts did his best to look stern in front of his daughter; it wasn't easy. After wiping away the tears from her eyes, Rebecca calmed down, slowly removed the tea towel and attempted a serious face. "She's in pain and has to take it easy, so we've agreed to take the kids till she can walk again."

"And poor Uncle Gary isn't old enough to take care of his own children?" she asked sarcastically.

"Well…"

"Uncle Gary couldn't start a fire with a flamethrower in the middle of a bonfire covered in petrol and firelighters!" interjected Sarah Roberts, narrowing her green eyes. Her husband blushed; his wife was right.

"Whatever his weaknesses, Sarah, he needs our help, OK? Rebecca?"

"OK!" Rebecca snapped in exasperation.

"They'll be arriving in the next couple of hours," he continued, "and Jasmine's going to share with you."

Rebecca groaned inwardly, then stomped up the stairs to tidy her room and hide her valuables away from Emily's grasping fingers: she hadn't returned her ring yet.

Two hours came and went rapidly and – surprise, surprise – Uncle Gary was on time. He was always on time when he needed a favour. And this was a major favour as far as Rebecca was concerned!

BRRINNGG!

"Open the door, Rebs!" called her father.

Heavily, she made her way down the stairs, counting them, mechanically, as she drew nearer and nearer the dreaded moment of…

"Alright, Becksy-Babes!" Uncle Gary gave her a whopping, wet kiss on the cheek; inside, she felt sick. He always gave wet kisses and she HATED 'Becksy-Babes'! What was he like? She wasn't a kid any more!

The rest of the hoard pushed past her. Jasmine ignored her; Emily avoided her eyes and kept her hands behind her back; Jamie waved another matchbox in her face and grinned. Her father gave his brother-in-law a brief hug.

"They'll be fine with us, don't worry,"

"Oh, I ain't worried, Terry, boy. I trust yuh. I 'preciate the 'elp: what, with Leanne in hospital and I've got so much work on…" Uncle Gary shook his head, sadly.

"Yeah, yeah, no problem, Gary," replied Terry Roberts, not commenting on the fact that when Sarah Roberts was in hospital for a minor operation, Gary and Leanne had been 'too busy' to cope with Rebecca for a couple of days.

"The roof building business ain't going to run itself, y'know?" Uncle Gary had said at the time. Nor would Terry Roberts' landscape gardening business run itself and so he lost several days of important work and a lot of money. But as usual he brushed over Uncle Gary's excuses – then and now. But he could feel Sarah Roberts behind him, bristling with anger.

"Don't let us keep you from visiting Leanne," Sarah Roberts said more loudly than she had intended. "Visiting hours aren't on much longer."

"You said you was going to watch the football on the telly, tonight, Dad!" shouted Jamie, gleefully.

"Wha'? Oh, no! You must've misheard me, Jamie, boy. I said I'd be visiting your Mum in the 'ospital, so I *wouldn't 'ave time* to watch the football on the TV, tonight." He looked uncomfortable. Jasmine looked daggers at him, but said nothing.

"Anyway, I better be off. Visiting hours, like you said, Sarah, an' Leanne with that crack on her coccyx. Be good you lot…" His voice trailed away as he realised that his children weren't listening to him. He nodded at Terry and Sarah Roberts and sidled out.

"Well," said Terry Roberts to the children, "what would you like to do, now?"

"I wanna go home!"

Rebecca rolled her eyes to the sky.

"Jamie, that's how you play the game…"

"But I want money!" Jamie started wailing.

"You lost it all because you landed on everyone else's properties..."

"Waaaaah!"

Rebecca looked, pleadingly, at her Dad.

"Give him some money from the bank," he said, "he's only little."

Where've I heard that before? Rebecca thought, angrily. *Aunt Leanne and Dad really are sister and brother.*

She handed over £500 to Jamie, whose greedy eyes lit up.

"I want more, too!" Emily piped up.

"Go on then," said Terry Roberts, pretty much knowing what was going to come next. He was right.

"Well if they're having more, then I want more, too!" Jasmine's green eyes flashed dangerously. Her Uncle Terry knew that look and didn't want to risk more strops and yelling. Jasmine in a temper was an awful sight. He handed both sisters £500.

"What about you, love?" he asked Rebecca, with a wary smile.

"No thanks. *Someone's* got to play this game according to the rules!" She gave her father a menacing grin.

The game lasted another hour. As Rebecca expected, Jamie quickly lost his money, but, despite his protestations – and to Rebecca's amazement – his sisters ganged up against him and refused to give him another 'loan'. He stormed off in a huff and mournfully tried to catch Uncle Terry's eye for sympathy; Uncle Terry ignored him. Rebecca suppressed a smile.

Emily went next as she tried to buy a house on Fleet Street, but instead got caught on Jasmine's hotel in Mayfair.

And then there were three. The competitors watched each other, intently: Rebecca sat, unblinking; Jasmine sat, unblinking; Terry Roberts sat, sweating. He was in a difficult position – his daughter on one side, his niece on the other. He would have to be completely even-handed. One hint that he was taking sides and his life would not be worth living. The two girls were rivals and deadly ones, at that.

"Come on, Dad. Throw the dice!"

"Uhh…actually, love, I just remembered. I've got to help your Mum with something in the kitchen. You two carry on and finish the game." He departed, rapidly, before she could challenge his lame excuse.

"All right 'Becks, your turn," smiled Jasmine, sweetly. The smile reminded Rebecca of a song that she could not quite recall; but she knew it was about a crocodile trying to lure its prey to its doom with its friendly grin. One wrong throw of the dice and she would be out. Amongst many others, Jasmine had hotels on Bond Street, Oxford Street, Mayfair and Park Lane! All the most expensive ones just waiting for Rebecca to land on. Rebecca, meanwhile, only had hotels on the Angel Islington, Old Kent Road and a house on Fleet Street. She shook the dice shaker, praying to land on 'Community Chest' and maybe win some much-needed cash. The dice clattered and bounced on the Monopoly board, scattering her hotels.

"Five!" yelled Jasmine, triumphantly, grabbing Rebecca's car and moving it straight on to Park Lane. "Gimme your cash!"

Reluctantly, Rebecca handed the last of her money to Jasmine. The bank had no money left so Rebecca wouldn't be able to pay her any more on a future throw. Jasmine shook the dice shaker and rolled them.

"Eight!" That put her just past Old Kent Road. Rebecca sighed. This was it. Only a miracle could save her now...

"All right, you two. Bed! It's half past ten!" It was Mum.

"No! I'm going to win the game!" screeched Jasmine.

"Finish it tomorrow."

Jasmine opened her mouth to argue, but shut it quickly. The icy gleam in Sarah Roberts' eyes said, 'Don't mess with me'.

Jasmine backed down, sulkily and rushed out of the room. Rebecca smiled gratefully at her mum and put away the board and its pieces into the box.

MONDAY

The next morning, Rebecca woke at 7.30. Jasmine was snoring quietly on the camp bed on the other side of the room.

Slipping quietly from under her duvet, her feet found her slippers. She tiptoed to the window and gazed out. White clouds, some blue sky, a hint of sunshine, no breeze…seemed like a good day to visit Ida.

Less than half an hour later, she was skipping out of the front door, around the pathway and through the gap in the trees that separated her pathway from Ida's.

"Hi Ida! I knew you'd be up early."

"Come on in, Becca. I've made a pot of tea already. Sit down over there. I'm just watching the news. Something terrible's 'appened."

Rebecca quickly sat down and began listening to the newsreader:

"Returning to our main story: a child has gone missing from a road in Lower Colbourne, a village in the east of Surrey…"

Rebecca turned towards her friend, her eyes widening.

"…at about 6.45pm, yesterday evening, Alice Denisov, 12, left her home in Blackberry Avenue, to visit friends in Sycamore Close…"

"Ida…that's just around the corner from here!"

"...Mrs Denisov received a call at 7.30pm from the mother of Alice's friend when she didn't arrive. The police have begun a full-scale search for Alice and house-to-house enquiries are currently underway. Inspector Paula Evers made this appeal to local residents:

'If you have seen Alice in the last 12 hours, please contact us so that we can piece together her movements. Mrs Denisov is desperately worried about Alice. Help from the public would be greatly appreciated and at this time we are very hopeful of finding Alice alive and well.'

"We will bring you more updates on this channel throughout the day..."

Ida turned the TV on to 'mute' and looked seriously at Rebecca.

"It's a terrible thing when young children go missing. You never know what's 'appened. That poor woman must be worried sick."

"Do you think the police will find her? Ida?"

"I don't know. It's all happening again...just like all those years ago."

Rebecca looked at her, closely. Confusion spread across her face.

"Again?"

"Yeah. I–I don't want to talk about it right now, Becca, if you don't mind."

They continued drinking their tea in silence and watched the rest of the news report. When it finished, there was an awkward silence. Rebecca felt uncomfortable. It had never been like this with Ida, before.

"My cousins are staying with us for a few days..." Rebecca began.

"Are they?"

"Yes and you can imagine what it's like at home with those three. It's a real nightmare!"

"Oh." Ida's gaze seemed distant, as if her mind was somewhere else. Rebecca realised that she was in the way.

"I'll see you later, then," called Rebecca as she slowly headed for the door.

"Yeah, all right, love," replied Ida, only half aware that her young guest was leaving.

Stepping outside, Rebecca closed the front door and began walking slowly to her house.

Reaching her own front door, she stood there, oblivious to everything, deep in thought, pondering the situation. She could understand why Ida was upset about the missing girl: who wouldn't be? But she seemed to be taking it so personally. Why had Ida been so mysterious? What happened so long ago? And why didn't she want to talk about it?

"Are you all right, Rebecca?"

Rebecca jumped, her door keys falling on to the path. She had been standing at her doorway for several minutes, staring into space, unaware of anyone or anything around her.

"I think she's in another world, Carl," came another voice.

"I reckon you're right, Cal," said the first.

Rebecca turned round, her cheeks reddening.

"Hi, Mr Jenkins. Hi, Mr Samuels. I was… daydreaming."

Carl Jenkins gave a small, understanding smile. His pale blue eyes crinkled at the corners of his eyelids as he glanced at his companion, while his wispy, grey hair, with a few blond strands, flicked back and forth in the gentle breeze. His right forearm leant casually against against Rebecca's front gatepost – which seemed barely strong enough to hold his powerful frame – while a gold watch sat upon the wrist of his left hand, which in turn rested upon his hip.

"Something on your mind?" he asked.

"Oh…one or two things. I…uh…was just thinking about that girl who disappeared last night."

"Worrying. Very worrying," frowned his companion, Caleb Samuels. "It never would've happened in my day. In Trinidad, everybody knew everyone else's business and trusted each other."

His eyebrows drew together more tightly as he went deeper into his memory, his right hand thoughtfully rubbing his short goatee, its few white hairs amongst the multitude of black ones, belying his sixty-plus years, while wrapped around his wrist, a gold, chain with his initial between the flat links, glittered in the sunlight.

"When we were kids we could go out any time with our friends and we were totally safe. Y'know, we used to climb palm trees by the beach in our bare feet and think nothing of taking the coconuts from the top branches, sometimes over 50 feet up. That's over fifteen metres, to you, Rebecca."

Rebecca's mouth fell open, though she guessed by his physique, showing through his navy-blue polo shirt, that he must still be very strong and his deep brown, unlined skin, gave him the appearance of a much younger man. He grinned at her.

"Yeah…we were always out and about in the sunshine, or even the rain! It was heavy, but never lasted long. We used to dry off in just a few minutes when the sun came back out. Our parents never worried about us. It was real safe. Everybody always watched out for each other."

"Yep," cut in Carl Jenkins, "You know, as a small boy I used to go into the forest with the other kids, play football in the street and go on errands, by myself, to the shops, to buy bread, meat...and even cigarettes for my Mum!"

"Cigarettes?" Rebecca was shocked. "Your Mum sent you to buy cigarettes when you were a little boy?"

Carl Jenkins and Caleb Samuels laughed at the incredulous expression on Rebecca's face.

"Well, people didn't realise how dangerous cigarettes were in those days and the law was different, then. Anyway, our parents always knew we'd be fine. But today...you can't walk down a street without fear of being insulted by anti-social teenagers, or mugged by drug addicts...and as for young children...well, these days I'm frightened for their safety when they're allowed out on their own." His wry smile had been replaced by a deep frown that mirrored the one on Caleb Samuels' face.

"I wish I could've been a child then," said Rebecca, empathetically.

"Ah well, times change. Just distant memories, now, eh, Cal?"

"Nahh. Seems more like yesterday, to me," replied Caleb Samuels in his warm, Caribbean burr. "You're only old if you think you are. And personally, I think I'm twenty-five years old; but, Carl, you're definitely an old man!"

Carl Jenkins roared with laughter and gave his companion a friendly slap on the back.

"Heh-heh," laughed Caleb Samuels. "You just look after yourself, young lady. Keep safe."

The two friends gave her a wave as they headed back to their homes, deeper into the Close. Rebecca returned the wave and then, turning back towards her wood-panelled front door, took out her key and entered the house. She leant her back against the door as she shut it, enjoying the cool air of the porch. It seemed to have been a long day already, yet it was still only 9am!

The kitchen was unusually quiet when Rebecca entered. Her cousins were already seated at the round, pine table. Jamie's legs dangled from the seat while Emily, scratched her fair, curly hair. Jasmine's back was towards her. Sarah Roberts looked up as she came in.

"Where've you been so early on a Bank Holiday Monday?" she queried.

"I couldn't sleep so I've been next door with Ida. Why, Mum?"

"Didn't you hear the news? About the missing girl?" Anxiety was playing across her mother's face.

"Yes. It happened really close to our road, just..." began Rebecca.

"What you don't know," said Sarah Roberts, lowering her voice and taking her daughter to one side, "is that she is a good friend of Jasmine's." As Rebecca crossed over to the table with her mother, she could see Jasmine's tear-stained face and reddened eyes. Her gaze was downcast and she looked somehow smaller, vulnerable and even pitiful. For the first time in her life, Rebecca felt sorry for her. She went over to her and laid her hand gently on her shoulder.

"I'm so sorry, Jaz. I had no idea. Where do you know her from?"

Jasmine looked up, sharply.

"What do you care?" She raced out of the room and up the stairs to Rebecca's room. Emily and Jamie stared at each other, not certain what was going on.

"Come on, you two," said Sarah Roberts, "help me to make some pancakes for breakfast."

"Yay!" they chimed together, dashing from their chairs and into her arms, nearly knocking her over.

Rebecca smiled at her Mum. She had a knack of knowing what to say and do at just the right moment. Sarah Roberts grinned at her daughter and nodded towards the stairs. Returning the nod, Rebecca strode across the kitchen and upstairs to her room. After gently tapping the door, she went in.

Jasmine was draped across the camp bed, face down, silently sobbing. Rebecca touched her shoulder. A muffled noise came from her cousin, which Rebecca translated, mentally, as 'leave me alone'. She persisted.

"Jaz…" Both Jasmine's hands began clenching, convulsively, as Rebecca began speaking. "…I know we haven't got on with each other in the past, but…"

Jasmine sat up so unexpectedly that Rebecca jerked back, involuntarily. Teetering on the edge of hysteria, Jasmine's words flew like cannonballs in Rebecca's face. "She's my friend: the *only* friend I've got. But I'm stuck here with *you* and I can't help her and I *hate* you!!"

Rebecca blanched.

"Hate me? Why?"

"Why? WHY? You know why! 'Look how slim Rebecca is. *She* always does well in the school sports. What a gymnast! Pity you ain't *taller*. Why don't you lose some weight? Can't you get on the netball team?' Sound familiar, does it, *Rebecca*?" She spat the name out. "That's my Dad whenever you're around, *always* comparing us. You've 'eard him!"

"ALL RIGHT!" yelled back Rebecca. "I've heard him; but it doesn't mean I agree with him!"

"So why didn't you say something?" Jasmine's face was contorted with rage. "Not even once?"

"I–I–I don't know. He's your Dad and I didn't want to get involved…"

"Yeah, you 'didn't want to get involved'. You could've helped me, *cousin*!"

Rebecca was aghast. She never expected this. Shame clambered up through her chest, into her neck and burned her cheeks. She couldn't meet Jasmine's gaze.

"You're right, Jaz. I never thought about it like that. I–I'm sorry. I…"

"Forget it!" Jasmine turned away, quickly; but Rebecca thought she heard a note of regret in Jasmine's voice.

BRRIINNG!

The doorbell.

Downstairs she could hear her Mum talking to someone. Muffled voices rose up the stairwell. Then it went quiet. Intrigued, Rebecca got up from Jasmine's bed to check who was downstairs. Suddenly, the bedroom door flew open. Mum looked serious.

"Girls, it's the police. They want to talk to all of us. Now!"

Waiting in the Roberts' family room stood two police officers: one older, male officer, the other, a younger, female officer. Rebecca and Jasmine entered nervously.

Though Rebecca knew they were completely innocent, she always felt a pang of guilt whenever she saw the police. They were wearing the typical Surrey police uniform: a thick, black, stab jacket overlaying the equally black, short sleeve shirt, with the officer's chrome numbers on the epaulettes; solid handcuffs protruded from a pocket near the waist, while a mobile phone sat in another by the left shoulder, a coiled wire connecting it to the officer via an earpiece. The older officer with three stripes on his epaulettes beckoned them in to sit on the gold-coloured sofa. His slim face and prominent jawline were framed by his very short, dark hair, which had just a hint of silver by his temples. His light-brown eyes regarded the girls seriously. The female officer, meanwhile, was also slim with a tanned complexion; her jet-black hair was tied back into a small bun. But her very large, dark eyes, had a gentle, kindly demeanour, restoring some of Rebecca's confidence.

The older officer spoke first.

"I'm Sergeant Mike Smith from Colbourne Police Station and this is my colleague PC Aditi Sharma. We're going door-to-door in the neighbourhood. I'm sure you'll have heard by now about the missing girl."

Rebecca and Jasmine glanced at each other. Jasmine looked frightened.

"You found her?" she asked.

The officers looked at each other, momentarily confused.

"Have you found Alice? She's my friend! Is she dead?" Her voice rose, rapidly. "IS SHE DEAD?"

"N—no, no," the Sergeant stammered, briefly taken aback by her outburst. "We haven't found her, yet."

Rebecca's Mum moved quickly to comfort Jasmine. As her arm went around her shoulders, the girl cried out:

"Then what're you doing here? What's the POINT?"

"We've just come to make enquiries about any person who may have seen her …" interjected PC Sharma, her eyes full of compassion, "…and warn all the local children not to go out alone in the evenings, even if they aren't going far. We had no idea that you were friends. We didn't mean to upset you. Was she on her way to see you?" Jasmine shook her head and buried her face in Sarah Roberts' shoulder.

"Alice didn't know she was staying with us," explained Rebecca's Mum. "Jasmine and her brother and sister are Rebecca's cousins. Their mother is in hospital so we're looking after them for now,"

Sergeant Smith scratched his short, dark hair, uncomfortably.

"I see. Uh…sorry young lady…Jasmine. We're doing our best to find her."

"Has she been kidnapped?" asked Rebecca.

"We don't know for sure what's happened to her, right now. We're keeping all avenues of investigation open. I'm hopeful we'll get her back safe. I don't suppose you or any of your family…" he nodded towards Rebecca, "have seen anyone suspicious around here?"

Rebecca and her Mum shook their heads.

"In that case I don't think we need to disturb you any longer, Mrs Roberts."

Rebecca watched as her Mum led the two officers to the front door. Looking out of the window, she saw the two of them stop at the gate for a moment in discussion – Rebecca surmised – about which way to go next. Sergeant Smith took out a notebook and wrote in it.

Then they headed off in the direction of Ida's house. Fingers of apprehension gripped her as she remembered Ida's strange mood.

"I hope she's ok," she said to herself. Then she turned back towards her red-eyed cousin. "Come and have a cup of tea, Jaz."

TUESDAY

꧁

It was midnight. Rebecca lay in bed, staring at the luminous stars on her ceiling. She loved their gentle, ghostly glow. It always made her feel like a little girl, in awe and wonder at the size of the universe.

But not tonight.

Her cousin was in the other bed – she'd been asleep for about an hour. All day she'd sat around the house not speaking to anyone, except to nod or grunt if Sarah or Terry spoke to her. Not even Jamie or Emily could bring her out of herself, so they ran off to cause mayhem in other parts of the house. After ignoring all Rebecca's attempts to talk to her and sobbing on and off for an hour and a half with her face to the wall, she became exhausted and finally passed out.

Rebecca had never felt so uncomfortable and anxious in her life. First, her good friend Ida was acting very weird and wouldn't talk to her and now her cousin – whom she had never liked – had managed to make her feel guilty for not sticking up for her. And then *she* wouldn't talk to her either! Now Mum and Dad were walking on eggshells with Jasmine's mood and jumpy if Rebecca even glanced at the front door.

No way could she sleep!

Silently, she sneaked out of her bed, her feet feeling around for the warm, trainer-shaped slippers, nearby.

Slipping on her dressing gown, she crept downstairs so as not to disturb anyone in the house and noise-lessly unlocked the back door. Perhaps a wander around her garden staring at the real stars would help. She felt quite safe: her L-shaped house and the fences and walls that formed the boundaries to the other properties completely surrounded the garden. The only entry point was a heavy, locked, two-metre gate, with overgrown bushes allowing only a narrow gap above it.

Looking up, the sky was awash with stars – more than she had ever seen, or dreamed possible. She remembered one of her primary school teachers explaining that without the moonlight or streetlight pollution, you could see the entire sweep of the stars across the Milky Way. At that moment, her whole perspective changed: here she was, on this tiny speck of dust called 'the Earth', circling a medium-sized star at 60,000 miles per hour, at the edge of a star-filled galaxy, among billions of galaxies in an infinite universe…her problems suddenly felt very small.

The spell that the heavens had cast was broken by an odd, mechanical noise and a strange glow, low on the horizon, about thirty to forty metres from where she was standing.

She rushed over to the gate that separated the front and back of the house. Climbing lithely up the wooden, horizontal and diagonal beams, Rebecca poked her head through the gap between the top of the gate and the branches, straining to see from where the sound originated.

It was coming from 20, Pine Tree Close – her new neighbours' house! She swallowed hard. Her heart was beginning to pound in her chest as she felt a thrill of excitement and fear.

"What are they doing at this time of night?" she thought. "Shall I...*should* I go and have a look?"

A moment later, she discarded her dressing gown on the branches of a nearby bush and slipped over the other side of the gate, heading for the disturbance. The glow, which was now weaker, seemed to be emanating from the far side of the neighbours' house – a similar L-shape to her own house, except that theirs was considerably larger – while the mechanical sound had stopped. She considered her options: through the gate, or over the iron-spiked fence? Hmm...not much of a choice. She took hold of the ridged handle-ring again, wondering how to open the gate without making that terrible machine-driven commotion. The problem resolved itself when the grinding, jerking racket resumed. Immediately, she forced the gate open. As she made her way cautiously along the gravel path, she realised that the noise might suddenly stop and her footsteps would be instantly audible. Throwing caution aside, she raced down the pathway between the trees, past the huge, arched doorway to the corner of the house.

Abruptly, there was silence.

Desperately, she threw herself back up against the cold, white wall and hid in the shadows, breathing rapidly. She could hear voices – gruff ones – but not what they were saying. Edging her way along the wall, she peeked round the corner; ready to pull her head back at the slightest hint of danger.

Three figures – dressed in long, dark coats flapping gently in the rising breeze – stood gesticulating at something. Although they were fifteen metres away and silhouetted by the ghostly glow, she could still make out the 'creature' who had opened the door on Sunday. Rebecca shivered, uncomfortably as the breeze in her face cut through her thin T-shirt and leggings. The light, now pulsing, appeared to be connected to the other end of a long, coiled wire stretching from a power point at the side of the building.

"Try it again!" called the shortest of the three who seemed to be in charge. Rebecca had the impression from his voice that he was the eldest.

"Mmhmm," growled the 'creature'. He held up something rectangular and pointed it: the mechanised clamour started once again. She could finally see something attempting to move. It was a remote-controlled garage door that was bucking up and down jerkily, but obstinately refusing to lift itself completely. The group was growing irritated.

"Get it open and get *them* out of there!" the voice commanded. The noise stopped unexpectedly, with the door halfway open. The creature and the second-tallest figure bent down and stepped into the garage. Just then, Rebecca noticed that the figures were not alone. Two large rottweilers were standing behind them. They were fascinated, it seemed, by whatever was going on in the garage. Strange noises emanated from within. What were they? Squeals? Voices? Impossible to tell with the mechanical grinding from the garage door. The two figures began to emerge from the doorway, trying to pull something that was struggling against them...but what? If only she could see.

The breeze changed direction, blowing from behind her.

"Grrrrr!"

"Satan?" The leader grabbed the collar of the bigger of the two dogs, which was looking in Rebecca's direction and straining to get away. "What's up?"

With horror, Rebecca realised that the Rottweiler had caught her scent! "You smell something, boy? Intruders? Go get!"

Before he had even let go of the dog, Rebecca was already sprinting down the path. No more worries about stealth. There was a dog on her trail and she had no intention of being on the receiving end of those powerful jaws. The huge animal came round the corner at high speed – it skidded on the loose stones and crashed into the large pot plants and bushes near where Rebecca had stood just seconds earlier. It yelped, loudly.

Rebecca ignored it and carried on running for the gate. *Not far,* she thought. *Got to get there before that dog gets back on its feet.* The dog was much faster than she was, she knew that. She grabbed the gate with her left hand, using her momentum to whip around it and pull it shut as hard and fast as she could; it juddered to a halt about fifteen centimetres short of the gate's catch.

The Rottweiler picked itself up and headed after her, pounding up the path. Rebecca was almost across the road as it forced its muzzle through the narrow gap and began muscling its way out of the gateway.

Using every ounce of strength in her well-trained, athletic body, Rebecca maintained her rapid pace. A deep growl closed in on her. There were only seconds left. Everything seemed to move in slow-motion for Rebecca, making each moment crystal clear in her mind: the dog had just rounded the entrance of her house; blood was pounding in her ears; the back gate was looming just metres ahead; the dog was closing in on her; she shortened her stride and powered into a double-footed leap; the dog leapt at the same moment; her head and shoulders were through the gap above the gate as her hands grabbed the top bar in a reverse hold; the animal crashed into the gate, its head grazing her rising feet; the huge impact broke her grip and sent her over the gate in an uncontrolled somersault; she landed, heavily, in some low shrubs and bounced hard on to the patio flagstones.

"Ooofff..." she gasped, the wind knocked out of her. While she lay there, struggling for breath, she heard a scrabbling and frustrated whining at the solid gate. In spite of her weakened condition, she managed half a grin.

Not today, you don't, doggo, she thought to herself.

"Satan! Here!" a familiar voice ordered. Rebecca heard the dog's paws crunching, rapidly along the pathway shingle. "So," came the voice again, "you live here. Nice and close..."

The implied threat was more frightening than the dog. As his footsteps moved away into the distance she released the breath that she didn't know she was holding.

Picking herself off the floor, Rebecca limped along the patio, to the back door she had left only ten minutes earlier, stopping only to grab the dressing gown she had hung on the bush. Stepping inside, she gently closed the door. Her left arm and the top of her left leg were aching. She rubbed them and involuntarily groaned. The pain was terrible.

"Must've hit them when I landed," she thought, soberly. She padded into the utility room. Flicking on the light switch, she pulled up her sleeve. Her elbow was beginning to swell up. Immediately, she went to the freezer and grabbed two bags of frozen peas. Wrapping them in a couple of thin cloths, she pressed one firmly on the swollen joint with her right hand and the other against her leg with her left hand. She felt the relief of their healing cold. Breathing deeply, Rebecca leaned heavily against the cool wall. Suddenly, she felt strange: her breathing became shallower and faster, she felt dizzy and a wave of vibration seemed to be building up from the very core of her body. Within seconds, she was shaking. Her legs collapsed beneath her. She felt she had lost all control.

Ten minutes later, the shaking had dissipated and as the strength slowly returned to her body, she became aware that she was lying on the cold kitchen floor. Sitting up, she pushed hard against the wall with her back and her feet against the floor tiles. Gradually, painfully, she slid up to a standing position. Rebecca removed the bag of peas from her arm and hip and returned them to the freezer. She considered what had just happened. She had heard of shock from her dad who told her of a time when he broke his leg as a teenager, but had never understood or experienced it until now. It hit her that it must have been because of the narrow escape from the Rottweiler and the impact when she hit the ground. There had been no time to think about the danger or the pain while it was happening. But now, away from it, she realised just how close she had been to a vicious mauling – or worse!

"I must've been mad," she whispered.

Seven hours later, Rebecca awoke. No, something had woken her. She sat up, gingerly, her elbow and leg still sore. Jasmine was sitting on the end of her bed, looking at Rebecca, oddly.

"What's happened?" asked Rebecca, suspiciously.

"Where'd you go last night?"

"What d'you mean?"

"I'm not stupid!" said Jasmine, irritably. "I heard you shut the door about midnight and you didn't come back for a good half hour. When you bumped into my bed, I was going to ask you, but you got into bed and fell asleep really quick."

Rebecca looked away.

"Oh, I, uh, I couldn't sleep, so I went downstairs to read some magazines. Then I came up when I felt tired," she lied.

"Oh yeah? What were you doin' with the magazines? Having a punch-up?"

Jasmine pointed at the large, purple bruise on Rebecca's arm.

"Oh...that?" answered Rebecca, covering her injury. "Well...um...I didn't turn the light on at first in the family room and I whacked my elbow."

"Huh! Why are you lying? No wonder I can't trust you!"

"Oh...no...I..." stuttered Rebecca, trying desperately to think of a way of rescuing the situation. "It's just that..."

"WHAT?"

Rebecca sighed.

"OK! I'll tell you." She used her most serious voice on Jasmine. "But you can't tell anyone else!" Jasmine raised her eyebrows in surprise, then nodded in agreement.

For the next few minutes, Jasmine was agog, cross-legged, elbows on knees and hands supporting her face, as Rebecca told her about the new people who had moved in, how she and Ida had gone to say hello and the weird encounter with 'the creature'.

Then she related the events of the previous evening and how she ended up standing within a short distance of the neighbour's garage where something strange was going on. When she described her narrow escape from the Rottweiler, Jasmine's mouth fell open.

"Bloody hell!" she exclaimed. Rebecca gave a tired smile.

"Yeah…bloody hell!" she agreed.

"Hey," Jasmine sat up straight, "wha'd you think them noises was in the garage?"

"Dunno exactly," admitted Rebecca, "but, scraping? Maybe…squealing?" Jasmine's eyes opened wider.

"Squealing? What type of squeals?"

"What?" Rebecca looked puzzled.

"What type of squealing? Animal? Human? WHAT?"

"I…I couldn't tell. It was too far away in the garage and there was too much noise from the men for me to hear properly. Why do you…?" She stopped, suddenly. "No! You don't mean…?"

"Yeah I do."

"You think that they might have…"

Jasmine nodded, solemnly. Rebecca went pale.

"And I was there. I might've been, I…I mean I could've been…"

"Yeah. I reckon you was lucky," said Jasmine.

"So what shall we do?" asked Rebecca.

"We get your Mum to call the police, for us," replied Jasmine.

"Mum? Oh no, we can't!" Rebecca's pale face became almost white with fear. "She'll ask us why and then I'll have to tell her that I was outside at midnight. She'll kill me!"

"Get a grip! It's better than my friend being kidnapped and hurt by some weirdos across the road, isn't it?" Jasmine's expression was torn between ferocity and fear. "You've gotta tell her now! Before it's too late!" Rebecca knew she was right. What was a telling off from her Mum compared to the missing girl's life? *She could be in that garage*, she thought to herself. Taking a deep breath, Rebecca asked:

"Will you come with me, Jaz?" A look of surprise crossed Jasmine's face. Then something happened that Rebecca could never remember happening – ever. Jasmine smiled at her! A genuine, natural, wide-toothed smile. And Rebecca realised for the first time in her life, just how pretty her cousin really was. She responded by doing something she had never done before in *her* life. She took hold of Jasmine's hand and returned the smile.

"Let's do it!"

Mum surprised Rebecca. She sat silently and listened to everything that her daughter and niece had to say. When they had finished speaking, Sarah Roberts got up, slowly, paced up and down the wood flooring for a few moments and then stopped. When she turned round, her brow was furrowed and her lower lip was between her teeth. She seemed to be trying to make a difficult decision. Finally, she spoke.

"If I understand you, these neighbours were behaving suspiciously and you already found them to be pretty creepy. You want me to phone the police based on what you think could have been the sounds of a child, squealing in the garage, so the police will get a search warrant and search their house and maybe arrest them for kidnapping. But if you're wrong about them..."

"Mum, how can you say that? Their dog nearly ate me up for din..."

"Be quiet!" snapped her mother. "I'm talking and I'm also trying to think what I should do to punish you for being so stupid last night!" Rebecca fell silent.

"Please, Aunt Sarah. Please call the police. It could be my friend. She could get murdered!" A single tear slid slowly down her cheek.

"All right!" Sarah Roberts noticed the wet trail on her niece's face. "All right," she said more softly, "but I hope we're not getting our new neighbours into trouble for nothing!"

Sergeant Smith was standing in the kitchen of 4, Pine Tree Close with PC Sharma listening, solemnly.

"Tell us exactly what you saw," coaxed PC Sharma. "Did you see a child?"

"Well, no, not really, but the noises in the garage were strange and I couldn't be sure what they were. The whole thing was really creepy and...I–I didn't see a child."

"Did you hear a child's voice cry out?"

"No – well, yes, but it was more like strange squeals...I–I don't know!" Rebecca sat down heavily, scowling, frustrated at her inability to give an accurate description. "That was when they set the dog on me. I didn't see or hear anything after that."

Sergeant Smith cleared his throat.

"Before I say anything else, young lady, you must understand that what you did was wrong and dangerous. Wrong, because you were trespassing on someone else's property; dangerous, because you put your life at risk. You really scared your mum. It's not easy being a parent: I've got a couple of my own kids and I worry about them even when I know where they are."

"Sorry," replied Rebecca, pink with embarrassment. "I was...curious."

"Hmmm. Look," he said, turning to Sarah Roberts, "we don't have enough evidence to get a search warrant, Mrs Roberts..."

Jasmine's face dropped and she let out a moan.

"*but*...he continued, "we can *ask* them if they'd mind showing us their garage which we are doing all over the district, due to new information we've received about the missing girl. We'll put them off your scent by going to all their neighbours and asking to see in their garages, too. If these people refuse, that'll be an indication that they're hiding something. *Then* we can ask a magistrate if we can have a search warrant. There's no guarantee, we'll get it, but it's possible."

Lunchtime came and went slowly for Rebecca. She was brooding in the large, dark leather armchair that nestled in the corner of the double-aspect family room, staring at the sun-drenched rhododendron branches, revealing and hiding her view of the Close in the breeze. Why hadn't the police contacted them with news? Waiting was so frustrating. She chewed on her lip – a trait of the females in the Roberts family.

She needed to talk to someone. But who? Mum was busy in her upstairs office, answering e-mails for her accounting business. Dad had taken her cousins to see their mother in hospital. There was only one person: Ida. Would she be willing to talk? Or would she clam up again, like the day before? Enough thinking. Leaping out of her chair, Rebecca rushed to the kitchen, grabbed a packet of chocolate biscuits and dived out of the front door.

As she reached the pavement, she glanced across the road. She froze in mid-step. A lone figure was standing, watching her in the shadows of the pine trees, next to the huge, iron gate. A long plume of smoke filtered between the gates and the overhanging trees. The figure's right hand flicked the lit cigarette butt into the street. The left hand rested on the large head of a Rottweiler, whose eyes were fixed on Rebecca. Unnerved, she tore her gaze from them and continued her short journey.

"'Ello love!" The broad smile at the open door melted the memory of the grim pair from her mind. "Come in, then." It was a relief to see Ida adjusting her silver, curly hair, leading her down the corridor. She was being herself again.

"I was just having a cuppa tea. There's plenty for you."

It felt just like any other day sitting in Ida's living room; except, deep inside, she knew that it wasn't. She debated telling Ida all about her 'near death' experience with the Rottweiler, but decided it could wait; she wanted to know what had upset her.

"So, how's it going with your cousins? Getting on any better? Or are they still giving you the run around?"

Ida's expression had become more solemn, but there was still a twinkle in her eye.

"Hmm, well, yeah, you were right, it's not as bad as I thought it'd be. Mum and Dad are keeping Jamie and Emily out of my hair and they're stricter than my uncle and aunt, so they aren't giving me a problem…"

"But…?" Ida raised a quizzical eyebrow.

"But…Jasmine. Well, it's weird, but she and I had a big argument…no…more like she told me off big time 'cos she said I never stood up for her when her Dad teased her about her weight; but now we're getting on really well…"

"'Ow come?"

Rebecca knew this moment would arrive. How could she tell Ida about her near escape the night before without letting her know about the police coming to her house? Alice's kidnapping had depressed Ida and Rebecca did not want that to happen again; yet, it seemed unavoidable.

"I, um, I went for a midnight stroll in the garden…" Ida raised an eyebrow, "…because I couldn't sleep. I was thinking about how angry Jaz was, and how…" she looked away, uncertain of what to say next.

"How upset I was yesterday morning?" Ida interjected. Rebecca nodded without looking up. "Go on."

"So, anyway, I wanted to clear my head. That's when I heard a weird noise…"

Ida listened intently to Rebecca's tale, without interrupting her. When Rebecca had completed her recount, including all the details about the police, Ida rubbed her chin, thoughtfully.

"You didn't *see* a kiddie, then?" she said, suddenly.

"No," said Rebecca.

"Then you don't know if they did it."

"Well, no."

"So you can't accuse them of kidnapping," said Ida, "no matter what your neighbours look or sound like …"

"But they set their dog on me!" exclaimed Rebecca.

"That's what guard dogs do, love. They protect. You were lucky. Those men didn't know it was a teenage girl who was there."

"But…" Rebecca's voice trailed away. Ida's eyes looked sombre and…and was that anger? But why? Rebecca squirmed, uncomfortably. "Ida, what's wrong? Have I upset you, or something?"

"Wha'?" Ida jerked in surprise and her expression changed completely.

"What's going on, Ida? The way you were looking at me, it was really scary. Did I do something that hurt you? Please tell me!"

Ida was focused again.

"N–no love, it–it's not you, it's something else. Something that happened…"

"Many years ago?" finished Rebecca.

"Yeah, love. *Thirty-five* years ago. I ain't spoken to anyone about it for such a long time."

"What happened? You can tell me anything, Ida. You know that."

Sighing deeply, Ida's hazel eyes turned back towards her young companion.

"Thirty-five years ago…I'd already been married for thirty years, near enough. I was so happy, then. Shahin and I used to travel a lot 'cos of his work and I was his personal assistant, so we went all over the world together, but 'specially the Middle East, where he was from. He was kind and gentle and he was so funny. We used to laugh so much. I'd say something that'd make him giggle, an' then he'd make fun of it and that'd crack me up; or he'd tell me a story from Iran which was so funny we'd be in fits, an' people would look at us as if we was mad! 'Ere, let me tell you a few." As she related some of the stories, Ida and Rebecca laughed and cried together, the stories were so comical. For several minutes, the two friends, separated in age by nearly seven decades, were united in helpless laughter.

As their giggles subsided, they wiped their eyes and slumped back in their chairs. Then their smiles faded as Ida began speaking again.

"Like I said, we was really happy together and it was near enough perfect, except, we couldn't have children. I don't talk…most people got no idea…I was pregnant, once y'see, but…I got hurt in a road accident and… lost the baby. Doctor said I couldn't have any more: we cried for a week. That was the saddest thing in our marriage…till thirty-five years ago, that is. That's when our lives was destroyed."

Rebecca was oblivious to everything except Ida's voice. What could possibly have wrecked their lives?

"There was a lovely girl that used to live just round the corner from where we are now: Catherine – not much younger than you are. We was friends with her Mum and Dad, Julie and David, 'cos I'd known Julie's family since she was a little girl. They'd come round our house regular like. Julie was like a little sister to me and Catherine was like our daughter.

"But then, one day, she went missing. Julie and David was frantic. They went all round the houses looking for her and we searched as well. Shahin drove all over the district: first one road, then another and another, real systematic he was. He didn't leave a street out for miles around. And he knocked on every door on every street. Sometimes people was sympathetic and sometimes they was rude. But he was always a gentleman to them.

"Then it happened."

"What?" said Rebecca, dreading the answer.

"About three days after she went missing, we had a knock on our door. The police. Someone'd tipped them off that someone had been seen offering Catherine a lift before she went missing. That someone said it'd been Shahin. The police took him in to 'help them with their enquiries' they called it. They kept him for two days, badgering him with questions and threatening him with being put in jail for life if he didn't tell 'em what he'd done to poor Catherine. Well, he denied all the charges and told them we loved her. They weren't convinced but they couldn't keep him any longer without charging him and they couldn't do that without evidence. So they let him go.

"His name should've been kept private, 'cos he hadn't been charged, but 'someone' leaked his name to one of the national newspapers and they put his name and picture on the front page as the *only* suspect for the kidnapping!

"Well, that was that. The papers and TV was camped on our doorstep for the next three weeks. Every move, Shahin made was watched. They rang our bell, banged on the door and phoned us all hours of the day and night, trying to get a story. We pleaded with them to leave us alone. We told them that we loved Catherine and she was like our own daughter. But they started using his nationality against him."

"Why, Ida?" asked Rebecca. "What was so terrible about where he was born?"

"Well, love, that'll take a bit of explaining. Let me see," Ida thought for a few moments. "It was the early 1980s and the British papers hated Iran, 'cos of a revolution they'd had a couple of years before. They threw out their Shah – that's their name for their king – and a revolutionary religious government took over. The old king had been friends with Britain, but the new Iranian government hated Britain."

"How come?" queried Rebecca.

"I asked Shahin about that. It was all about oil. Seems the British secret service was working hand-in-hand with the American CIA to get rid of the Iranian government in the 1950s. The oil belonged to Iran, but the British and the Yanks were controlling it and taking too much money out. So, the Iranian government threw them out and took back control of their oil and the money.

"Now the Shah didn't like his own government, see, 'cos the prime minister just wanted the Shah to be a figurehead. You know: no power of his own to rule – just stand up in his royal robes and look good for the country! So, when the British and American secret services got rid of the Iranian government, they made sure the Shah got the power he wanted, just so long as he supported the UK and the US. But lots of the Iranians hated the Shah for being a puppet-king for the West.

"As soon as the Iranian people got rid of the Shah in 1979, the new government started causing problems for Britain and America, as revenge."

"But how did that get Shahin into trouble?" inquired Rebecca.

"Well," sighed Ida, "some of the papers started saying Shahin was connected to the Iranian government and that they were all terrorists who hated British people and…" Ida paused, barely able to say the next words, "… kidnapping innocent kiddies was the sort of thing they did!"

"Oh Ida, that's terrible!"

"I know. But it didn't stop there. People we knew started avoiding us and soon, Julie and David did the same. One day, David even 'ad a big quarrel with Shahin on the street, accusing him of kidnapping Catherine…and worse!

"Strangers began to spit at him on the streets and…" her voice faltered, "…and he even got beaten up in the town centre, when he was coming 'ome from a prayer meeting.

"Then he lost his job. Oh, his company said they was making redundancies 'cos of the 'economic recession'! But no one else in the company got fired and two weeks later someone new took his job!"

Rebecca was now kneeling down in front of her friend, holding her hand, tightly. How could people behave like this? And adults, too! She knew what *school* could be like when rumours started spreading – it didn't take long for a bit of fanning to make a small lie turn into something big and nasty. It'd happened to a friend of hers: subtle bullying at first, then isolation, rumours and cyber-bullying – it went on for months. Eventually the family moved away to another town and school many miles away. Rebecca had felt so helpless and angry. But those were *children*; how could grown-ups do it?

"I'm so sorry, Ida. Why are people so cruel?"

"Prejudice, all of it. Prejudice! They never 'ad a shred of proof, but still they kept hounding him. Then he–he became depressed: I mean *really* depressed. My lovely, kind, funny Shahin...he lost his smile, he wouldn't eat, he hid himself away at home and he didn't even want to get out of bed. The weight just dropped off 'im and he never had much to begin with! I tried everything to bring him out of it, but I couldn't!"

"Then, one day, we was at 'ome, having a cuppa tea, when...he...he collapsed on the floor. He just stopped breathing. I called 999 and I tried the kiss of life but...nothing. He was dead. Just like that, he was dead!" Her narrow, frail shoulders shuddered as she cried uncontrollably. "I couldn't save 'im Rebecca. I couldn't help the man I loved!"

Rebecca flung her arms around Ida, trying to comfort her; but her own tears burned in her eyes with indignation for her beloved friend...and a man she had never met.

That evening, Rebecca sat at the dinner table, pushing her vegetables and chicken Kiev, aimlessly, around her plate. Jamie and Emily were chatting excitedly.

"Mum wants to come home!" shouted Jamie.

"The doctor says Mum's gotta stay till Friday. She 'ates 'ospital food," said Emily, grinning.

"I gave her a big hug," Jamie continued, "then she screamed."

"That's 'cos you jumped on her, Jamie!" interjected Jasmine.

"I didn't jump on her, I jumped on the bed and I tripped on the blankets..."

"…and fell on her!" came Jasmine's increasingly irritated voice.

"I tried to get Jamie off the bed, 'cos Mum was yelling!" shouted Emily.

"Yeah, she yelled even more when *you* landed on her!" Jasmine shook her head, while Sarah and Terry Roberts made eye contact and tried hard to look serious.

Rebecca, oblivious to the conversation, continued chasing a line of sweetcorn around the white, blue-rimmed plate with her fork. Jasmine looked over at her.

"What's up?" she enquired.

"Mmm?" replied Rebecca, not lifting her eyes from her sweetcorn train.

"You ain't said a word since we got back. Talk to me!" hissed Jasmine, trying not to alert her Aunt and Uncle who were engrossed with Jamie and Emily's hospital chatter.

Rebecca slowly raised her eyes.

"Not now. After dinner. In the bedroom," she whispered.

Jasmine gave a small nod in acknowledgement, then returned to her younger brother and sister.

"Mum says she's hurt her cock-a-doodle-doo!" called out Jamie.

"No, her cop-sticks!" shouted Emily, in outrage.

"Her coccyx, you dummies!" laughed Jasmine. And even Rebecca had to smile.

An hour later, the two cousins escaped to Rebecca's room and became engrossed in conversation. Jasmine immediately picked up on certain points of Rebecca's story.

"So, this old lady…"

"Ida," said Rebecca.

"Yeah…Ida. Anyway, she reckons her husband never hurt that girl, yeah?"

"Of course he didn't, he was a really nice guy…"

"So *she* says. But how'd *you* know that for sure?"

"Well, because I trust her and if you heard her, you'd know she was telling the truth," said Rebecca, determined to make Jasmine believe her. "They kept attacking Shahin and it killed him!"

"Okay, maybe it's true, maybe she's right an' he was a good person. Which means he didn't kidnap the kid, which means…?"

"Which means someone else did!" exclaimed Rebecca.

"Exactly!" grinned Jasmine. "You want everyone to know that Shahin was innocent, right?"

"Right!"

"Then we gotta prove it."

"Us?" Rebecca's eyebrows shot up in surprise.

"Yeah. *Us!* The police ain't interested in what happened thirty-five years ago, so they won't investigate it. But we can." Jasmine lay back on the bed, her elbows propping her up. "All we've gotta do is work out what questions to ask and who to get the answers from."

"Yeah, right," said Rebecca, cynically, "sounds easy, but we're not detectives. What can we do that the police couldn't do back then?"

Now it was Jasmine's turn to raise her eyebrows.

"Don't you know nothing? Two things on our side: one, we ain't gonna put the blame on Ida's husband just 'cos he's from another country, like they did back then."

"And second?"

"And second...the internet didn't start till years after their investigation; but we've got it and we'll use it to get some answers."

Jasmine's enthusiasm made Rebecca beam; but only for a moment.

"Jaz, it's really great of you to help me like this, but what about *your* friend? Wouldn't you rather do something for her?"

Jasmine winced.

"Course I would! She's my best friend. My only *real* friend..." It was Rebecca's turn to wince. Jasmine caught her pained expression and nudged her. "...until today. But now," she said, her head hanging, "she's... dead...murdered!"

"We don't know that!" said Rebecca.

"Yes we do! 'Ow many missing kids end up alive after they go missing?"

Rebecca was about to answer, then she stopped.

"I–I don't know," said Rebecca.

"Not bleedin' many!"

"But we can't just give up, Jaz! I'm sure those new neighbours are behind it. Maybe if we went there again..."

Jasmine cut her off.

"And get eaten by them dogs? Gimme a break!" She paused for breath. "The police are checking *them*, so let them get on with it. We can keep busy by solving our own mystery. Together." She paused again. "I...I ain't got many friends and I don't wanna lose Alice, 'cos we been together since nursery. But it's killing me to think of her. I wanna do SOMETHING to keep busy. An' if we can't help the police find *her*, maybe we *can* help Ida," she said with fierce determination. Rebecca nodded. The police would find the evidence to arrest the neighbours...and hopefully rescue Alice at the same time.

"Where do we start?" asked Rebecca.

"Hmm. Talk me through the story again, cuz."

WEDNESDAY

꧁꧂

"What's got into you two?" queried Sarah Roberts, at the breakfast table.

"Hmm?" the girls chorused, innocently, a bit of cornflake sticking out of the side of Rebecca's mouth and milk dribbling down Jasmine's chin. "You've been chattering away nonstop for the last 15 minutes!"

They turned, looked at each other, noticed the mess on each other's face and immediately started giggling.

Sarah Roberts smiled. She had never seen her daughter and niece getting on so well. Maybe it was Alice's tragic disappearance that had thrown them together.

Misery acquaints a man with strange bedfellows, she thought to herself. "Now where on earth did that phrase spring from?" she said out loud.

After helping Mum clear away the dishes and the cereal boxes, they dragged a protesting Jamie and Emily into the bathroom, threatening them with a visit to the dentist that morning if they didn't brush their teeth. Ten minutes later, disgruntled and confused, the two siblings ran out of the bathroom and headed for the garden – the safest place to be away from this new dynamic duo of Jasmine and Rebecca.

"S'not fair!" shouted Jamie.

"Yeah!" agreed Emily, brushing her hair behind her left ear. They're being horrible to us. They're bullying us. Why's Jazzy being nice to Becksy?"

"Dunno," replied Jamie, wiping his runny nose on the sleeve of his blue jumper. "Let's look for worms!"

"Yeah an' put them in their beds!" said Emily, venomously.

"Not gonna play with them any more!"

"Yeah, we'll just play with each other, Jamie." After sealing their pact with a high five, they began looking in earnest for worms.

Rebecca and Jasmine pored over her laptop.

"So, do we know when she was kidnapped?" asked Jasmine.

"Not exactly, but it was *about* thirty-five years ago," replied Rebecca.

"Right, so put 'child kidnapping' an' the year." Rebecca did as instructed. A range of links appeared, rapidly on the screen. After scanning over several pages and checking several possible leads, Jasmine shook her head.

"God, it's all so sad," said Rebecca. "So many children kidnapped. Why do people do it? And those poor parents. They all felt guilty…But it wasn't their fault…I mean, they couldn't watch their kids 24/7. How were they to know that some paedophile…?"

"It's all from America," Jasmine said, cutting her off. "None of this stuff is any good to us. We gotta narrow it down. Try putting in 'UK' at the end." Rebecca nodded, then entered the new search words – new results appeared.

"Let's see what we've got. 'Parental Kidnapping'? What the hell's that?" Rebecca and Jasmine scanned the information from the link at the top of the page. "Oh. It's a special agency that brings back children who've been taken abroad by one parent after they've split up, divorced or whatever, without getting permission from the other one."

"Never 'eard of that before," said Jasmine. "But that's not what we want. There's got to be something about that girl. Just a minute…Catherine wasn't it? Try that link, there. Yes!"

On the screen was a report, detailing the known events surrounding the young girl up to the time of the kidnapping.

Rebecca began reading aloud:

"It says:

'The 2nd June seemed like just about any other early summer's day in Colbourne Village. Catherine Rayburne, nine years old, was waved off at approximately 4.15pm by her mother, Julie Rayburne of 134, Ash Close, to go to the local shopping parade, a half a mile down the road. This was a trip she had done once a week, for many months. Yet this was to be the last.

"Katie was a nice kid. Always polite when she came into my shop," said retired mini-supermarket owner John Bradley. "She bought milk, eggs and sugar for her mum to bake a cake and then for herself, lemon sherbet, liquorice strings, a bar of chocolate, and comics. Last I remember when she left was her lovely smile and a wave goodbye. I was shocked when I heard she'd been taken."

She then visited her friends at 24, Pine Tree Close...

The girls stared at each other.

"Your road!" exclaimed Jasmine. Rebecca nodded and then returned to the article.

...where she stayed for an hour or so, playing with her friends, Jeremy and Laura Clark. She was last seen heading back up Pine Tree Close at about 6.15pm. No one spotted her walking along Devon Street, the main road that led back to her cul-de-sac. Police have assumed that Catherine was probably abducted before she could reach the road.

Her parents, David – an architect from New Perspectives Partners – and Julie – an infant teacher in Colbourne Junior School – went on TV to plead for her safe return just two days after the disappearance; a plea that was ignored by the kidnapper.

Surrey Police spent months investigating Catherine's case, including interviewing all the local residents of Pine Tree Close.

Only one person seemed to come under close scrutiny and that was Mr Shahin Dehmobedi, a resident of Pine Tree Close. He was interviewed several times, but no solid evidence was ever uncovered. Mr Dehmobedi always maintained his innocence, in spite of a major campaign led by some of the national tabloid newspapers against him. Mr Dehmobedi died of natural causes just a few months after Catherine vanished.

No new individuals were ever interviewed; leading many to believe that the Police felt their only real suspect had gone. The case was closed, finally, two years later, with no new leads or evidence.

We may never know whether or not Mr Dehmobedi was the kidnapper, as Catherine's body has never been recovered, although there were no clues to indicate that any other person was involved.

We can only feel sorrow for her parents and try to understand the guilt they felt and still feel, as any parent would who had to live with such a tragedy; their tomorrows never live because their yesterday never dies, as they can have no closure without knowing the fate of their beloved child.

As Mrs Rayburne so pitifully said: "I sent my child out to die that day, but I'll never be able to bury her".' Written by Lesley Stevenson from The National Herald, *in 2006.*

Rebecca sat back and sighed, heavily. "It doesn't look good for Shahin, does it?"

"No," said Jasmine, "but we can't give up that easily. Let's look at the article again."

The cousins combed through it, taking notes as they went. After ten minutes, Rebecca said:

"Well, we've got some names and two addresses."

"From thirty-five years ago!" Jasmine reminded her. "Prob'ly dead or moved away!"

"Yeah, but maybe one of them still lives there! Why don't we try to find out by asking some questions?"

"Now you're talking!" enthused Jasmine. "Let's do it!"

"Mum, Jasmine and I are going out for a while, okay?" Rebecca asked.

"Where are you going?" her Mum asked anxiously.

"Oh, just down the road and into the village…"

"Why?" Sarah Roberts's expression became very serious.

"We're…doing some research," blurted out Jasmine. "Becks asked me for some help!"

"Oh!" Sarah Roberts was taken aback by the revelation. "Well, that's great that you're both working together. I, uh, can't see any problem in you doing that, except that I want you back here by 5 o'clock."

"5 o'clock!" said the girls together.

"Yes, 5 o'clock!" Sarah Roberts repeated. "I trust you to be sensible, but I'm worried for your…I mean… well, after …you know…"

"We know, Aunt Sarah," said Jasmine, sympathetically. "You don't want us to get kidnapped, too. But there's two of us and we're thirteen, not nine, y'know."

"Don't worry Mum, we won't talk to strangers, or get into anyone's car!" A mischievous, lop-sided grin spread across Rebecca's face. It made Sarah Roberts giggle, in spite of the seriousness of the situation.

"All right, I get the picture! You're not babies any more! Just be back on time, or I'll send Emily and Jamie out to find you!"

"Oh no!" said Rebecca with a flourish of melodramatic arm gestures and exaggerated facial expressions. "Not that!"

"Get outta here!" A wet sponge flew past the ears of the laughing girls as they rushed out of the kitchen.

"Well done, Jaz."

"What for?"

"You managed to get Mum to let us go out without lying about it and without telling her the real reason for us going out."

"D'you think she'd mind?"

"I'm not sure," Rebecca's green eyes were pensive. "But I feel happier not worrying her with it. Let's try 24 Pine Tree Close, first. I wonder if the Clarks still live there? I don't really know anyone from that part of the Close. But I think there may be a couple of college students with their parents, there."

Marching round the corner of Pine Tree Close to their first port of call, the girls reviewed their questions.

"You nervous, Becks?"

"About what, Jaz?"

"Maybe people won't talk to us?"

"That doesn't scare me!"

"Nah, s'pose not. Just be careful what you say, OK?" Rebecca looked confused. "People 'ave feelings!"

They continued down the cul-de-sac past a group of large, semi-detached houses, until they reached a detached house on the left, surrounded by neatly trimmed fir trees. The pathway, leading in from an ungated entrance, comprised red and white blocks in geometrical patterns. At the end of it, a large, silver Mercedes and a small, blue VW Beetle stood outside the single garage.

The house itself appeared to have been recently redecorated: all the windows, gutters, drainpipes and fascia looked brand-new.

With Jasmine's warning still ringing in her ears, Rebecca approached the white front door a little more tentatively than she had a few moments earlier. Taking a deep breath and letting it out slowly, she pressed the doorbell. Almost immediately, loud voices could be heard from inside: "Bye! Bye! See you later! Byee!"

The door was pulled open by a fair-haired teenaged girl – older than the two cousins – in a pink crop-top, denim shorts and a bag slung across her shoulder. Her broad smile disappeared as she was confronted by the faces of Rebecca and Jasmine. "Oh! Oh! Uh, yes? Can I help you?" she said through a frozen, thin-lipped smile.

"Yes please," said Rebecca, taken aback at their unusual welcome, "we're looking for Mr and Mrs Clark. Do they live here?"

"Who? Clark?" she said. "No one here by that name."

She was about to close the door when Jasmine piped up: "They lived here before you 'n' your family. Maybe someone inside knows where they live now?"

The girl's eyes narrowed, her lips became tightly pursed.

"All right, I'll ask!" She slammed the door on them. The girls looked at each other, bemused. Thirty seconds later, the door reopened. "No. No one knows anything about them. The last people here before us were called Anderson – and we don't know where they live either!" she said quickly, just as Jasmine was going to ask for a forwarding address.

"Oh, OK," said Rebecca.

Suddenly the teenage girl's eyes lit up.

"He's here! Danny's here!" the girl called into the house. "Bye! Bye! See you later!" Then she slammed the door behind her, pushing Rebecca and Jasmine out of her way. The girls watched her back racing down the pathway to a tall, muscular young man who had pulled up outside the house in a classic mini with custom-built skirts and turbo. They kissed, jumped into the car and turbo-roared out of the Close.

Jasmine stared after them and shook her head.

"Let's try the next one," she said.

Ten minutes of brisk walking later, they reached Ash Close, a wide, tree-lined cul-de-sac with a large, grassy area, some fifty metres from the main road, where half a dozen young children were happily chasing each other around its leaf-laden ash trees.

"Number 134. That should be on the...right side of the road, near those children. Come on." Rebecca led the way, her cousin's shorter legs trying to keep up with her long, athletic strides, which ate up the ground beneath her. "126...128... 130...132...here we are: 134, Ash Road." Rebecca glanced at Jasmine, uncomfortably. "My hands are sweating," she said, wiping them on her jeans. "Why now?" She tried to lick her lips that were suddenly dry. She hesitated at the wooden gate with crumbling blue paint.

"Wotcha expect? We're about to meet the parents of the dead girl! You wanna back out?"

"I – I...no. Give me a moment. I'm just preparing myself for it. M–maybe we need more time..."

Jasmine's eyes flicked skywards.

"Come on Becks! Let's get it over!" She flung open the gate and marched in with Rebecca trailing in her wake, over the small red and white diamond-shaped tiles with grass growing through the gaps. As they reached the door, griminess and cracks in the whitewashed walls of the house became visible; the wooden window frames had blistering paint and the windows themselves were almost opaque with dirt. At the doorway there was no doorbell.

"D'you think anyone's in?" asked Rebecca, thinking the whole expedition was a really bad idea.

"'Ow should I know? Knock the bleedin' door!"

Her hand shaking, she tapped the glass, gently.

"Oh my God! Not like that! Like this!" Jasmine rapped hard upon the glass. They waited, expectantly, hardly breathing. Nothing. Jasmine rapped again, harder. This time, they saw the brief light of a door opening and closing in another part of the house. Then a figure, dim at first, came slowly to the door until a face peered out at them through the swirls in the glass of the door. A woman.

"Who is it?" came a quavering voice.

"H-h-hello. M–m–my name is R–R–R–Rebecca Roberts." Jasmine's eyes turned skyward again.

"And my name is Jasmine Bracewell."

"What do you want?" The voice sounded suspicious.

"W–we're trying to find Mr and Mrs Rayburne," continued Rebecca. There was a pause, then there was a rattle of the chain behind the glass, followed by a click. The door opened a crack for a few moments, then slowly it opened to reveal the owner of the voice. A tall, slender lady in her late sixties, with short, silver hair, stared at them through tired, dark brown eyes.

"I'm Mrs Rayburne. Why would you be trying to find me?"

"It's a long story," said Rebecca, "but it's very important. We need your help."

"With what?"

"A project. We're doing a local research project," interjected Jasmine.

Mrs Rayburne bit on her lower lip, as she looked them up and down, then gave a small smile.

"Perhaps you'd better come in," she said.

Mrs Rayburne led the girls into a large hallway where a wide, curving staircase rose up to a gallery. Her shoes' heels clicked on the dark, parquet flooring, in contrast to the girls' squeaking trainers. They came to a door with glass panels that she opened. The room was about six metres in each direction and was stuck in an early 1980s time warp: beige and brown coloured wallpaper with vertically joined, rounded hexagons; and a classic Parker-Knoll three-piece suite. The inside of the house echoed the condition of the outside of the house: slightly worn out and uncared for.

The girls were ushered on to the large, soft, golden-brown, sofa, while Mrs Rayburne perched upon the edge of one of the equally soft, golden-brown, armchairs. Jasmine turned to Rebecca and mouthed 'get on with it!'

"Well, Mrs Rayburne, you see, my cousin..." Rebecca indicated Jasmine with a glance, "thought that it would be a good idea if she...I mean *we* asked you a few questions." Her heart was racing as her mind tried to find a way to ask the inevitable questions without mentioning Ida's name. "We are investigating real-life stories for a project for school..."

Jasmine's eyes widened for a moment as she could see where Rebecca might be going with her story.

"Oh, you mean what life was like in school in the 1950s? I can tell you all about that..." began Mrs

Rayburne, happily, leaning back into her chair. "I was a child in the Fifties. Our classrooms were very different from what you have today. And technology? We had blackboards instead of those interactive whiteboards you have now. Computers didn't exist…"

"Yes, I'm sure that's fascinating, Mrs Rayburne, but um, well, no, not exactly…our project is on…um"

"The fact is, Mrs Rayburne," said Jasmine cutting in, "that our project is on a very serious subject. It's something that lots of kids are talking about in the neighbourhood and are really worried about, so we thought we should do a project for school on it an' help the kids to understand it an' know what to do an' how to behave if…"

"What *are* you talking about?" Mrs Rayburne looked baffled, the lines deepening between her eyebrows. Rebecca took over again.

"You've probably heard the news about the missing girl wh…"

Confusion was replaced by sudden suspicion.

"You're here to talk about a missing child? You think your school would want you to ask people questions… about a missing child?" Mrs Rayburne's face was changing colour, from its usual pallor to a deepening red that began rising from the bottom of her neck.

"Well," said Rebecca, swallowing hard, "not just *any* child…"

"You–you've come to my house to ask me questions about *my* child, haven't you?"

The pitch of Julie Rayburne's voice became higher and colour had reached her cheeks.

"MY CHILD! You've come into *my home* to ask me what happened to my lovely daughter, thirty-five years ago? To ask me what I did? To ask me how I felt! To ask me '*how I feel today*?'!"

Her body and her voice were both shaking. Rebecca gripped Jasmine's hand, tightly.

"No, Mrs Rayburne, we're trying to solve her disappearance and help...your friend...her husband was accused of kidnapping your daughter; but Mr Dehmobedi would never..."

"WHAT?" Julie Rayburne's eyes widened. "You've come to help that...that murdering, middle-eastern ba..." She stopped abruptly.

Her fists started clenching and unclenching, her knuckles showing white each time her hands closed. When she spoke again, her voice was unnaturally quiet. "My lovely Katie was murdered thirty-five years ago by that *brute*...and his wife helped him cover it up. They called themselves our friends but they were ravening beasts, preying on helpless children!"

"But Mrs Rayburne, Ida's not like that. She and Shahin loved your daughter..."

The woman jumped up suddenly, her face a white, stone bust of hatred, terrifying to behold. Even Jasmine was beginning to get scared.

"You *know* that woman? That *evil* woman? How dare you come into my house and question me. How DARE you come into my house! How DARE you! HOW DARE YOU!! DAVID!" She rushed to the living room door, screaming up the stairs. "DAVID!!!"

Footsteps thudded rapidly across the ceiling. A door slammed and the footsteps echoed in the upstairs gallery and then down the stairs. A few moments later, a strong, tanned, silver-haired man entered the room, with deep concern in his piercing blue eyes.

"What's wrong, Julie? What's happened?"

"David! They're asking about our daughter. OUR daughter! They're friends of that Iranian and his wife… make them go away. MAKE THEM GO AWAY!!"

"Go upstairs, darling. I'll deal with this." Mr Rayburne practically carried his wife to the foot of the stairs and watched her go step by faltering step up to the gallery. Then he returned to the girls. "I'm afraid you'll have to leave."

"But Mr Rayburne…" protested Rebecca.

"You'll have to leave, *now*!" There was authority in his voice, thought Jasmine, but no anger or hysteria like Mrs Rayburne. She grabbed Rebecca by the arm and hauled her back to the door. Mr Rayburne turned the latch and let them out. As they walked down the path, Rebecca suddenly turned round and fixed Mr Rayburne with a steady, unflinching gaze.

"He didn't do it, you know," she said, levelly. Mr Rayburne's gaze dropped to the floor.

"I know," he replied.

"You know?" Jasmine said, incredulously.

"Yes. I know. I've known for years." He looked behind him and partially closed the front door, afraid that his wife might hear him. "Look, I'm going in to the village tomorrow at ten in the morning. If you want to talk to me, we can do it then at the coffee bar, OK?"

The girls were too surprised to say anything and simply nodded. Then he went back into the house, shut the door and his shape receded on the other side of the glass door.

"Well," said Jasmine, scratching her head, "whatcha make of that?"

Rebecca didn't speak to Jasmine on the walk home; instead, she continually chewed her lower lip, shook her head, occasionally stopped in the middle of the pavement, groaned and threw her head back, staring at the sky. When Rebecca gave a particularly loud groan, Jasmine exploded.

"If you shake your head or bite your lip one more time, I'm gonna belt ya!" She grabbed Rebecca by the shoulders to face her. "What's your problem?"

Rebecca looked shocked. Unconsciously, she began to bite her lower lip; then she noticed the fire burning in Jasmine's eyes and stopped.

"I–I've been thinking."

Wha' about?"

"…Me…"

"Wha' about you?"

"'Till a few days ago, I thought…I thought I was a… nice person," said Rebecca. "I mean, I get on well with people and I don't quarrel with them or anything… but…"

"But what?" asked Jasmine.

"…but I don't think I *am* a nice person at all!"

"Why, Becks?"

"Because you were right. People *do* have feelings. And I was all ready to go in and tell the mother of a dead child that *I* think she was wrong about who killed her!"

"But she *is* wrong!"

"I know, Jaz, but she lost her daughter and I should've thought about that, too! All that sadness in her life and I dragged it up." Rebecca looked on the point of tears. Jasmine's arm went around her shoulder. "Then there's you…"

"Me?"

"Yeah, you. I used to think you were just grouchy and jealous..." Jasmine's arm dropped from her shoulder.

"Thanks!"

"I said I *used* to think that; but since you've been staying with us, I've really got to know you. And... you've been great." Rebecca smiled at her. "You've been a really good friend and you're funny, too!"

"Yeah? *Good* funny?" A lop-sided grin appeared on Jasmine's face.

"Yeah. Good funny. Jaz, *your* friend's gone missing, but you're still helping me so I can help one of *my* friends. I really appreciate it." Rebecca's hug took Jasmine's breath away. "Thank you *so* much."

Jasmine hugged her back.

"S'all right," she replied and closed her eyes. She needed to have the hug as much as Rebecca needed to give it – the last few days had been hard; and neither of their problems looked like being solved. When they separated, Jasmine was blushing.

"Alice has been my friend for years, but she's more like a little sister. Don't have any really close friends my age." She blushed again. "Thanks."

"What for?" Now it was Rebecca's turn to ask questions.

"For not just seeing me as some stupid, fat..."

"You're not stupid *or* fat."

"Fat compared to you!"

"You're *not* fat!" Rebecca was adamant.

"All right, I'm not. But I'm no good at sports: I can't run fast, I can't kick a ball, can't do gymnastics... and I'm not pretty...my Dad doesn't think..."

"No, your Dad *doesn't* think! That's the problem with him. And he's wrong about you. If he spent half as much time with you, Jamie and Emily as he does on watching football…" Rebecca stopped. She was beginning to sound like her Mum. "Sorry. He *is* your Dad."

"Yeah, well…He's all right sometimes. He's funny, too. Just doesn't know when he *isn't*. Doesn't know when he gets on my nerves, neither." Jasmine sighed loudly. "Come on, let's get back to the house."

As they rounded the tree-lined corner of Pine Tree Close, a police car was coming the other way. PC Sharma waved from the passenger seat and smiled at them as it went past.

"Hey, maybe there's some news about that search warrant!" exclaimed Rebecca. They raced down the middle of the road, desperate to find out the latest news.

"What do you mean, there's no search warrant!" Rebecca simply couldn't believe it. "Didn't they hear what I said about the noises in the garage and the dog chasing me?"

"Of course they did!" said Sarah Roberts, exasperated. "But the magistrate who signs the search warrant reckons there needs to be more evidence of wrongdoing before he can give it the ok."

"What does he want?" asked Jasmine. "Dead bodies?"

"No…just more than a few…impressions from… from a young girl!"

Rebecca's jaw dropped. Her cheeks turned crimson.

"I'm thirteen years old! I'm not just a little girl!" She paced the kitchen, slapping the kitchen tops, angrily.

"Calm down, Rebecca. You didn't let me finish. Sergeant Smith said that before he tried to get a search warrant he went to speak with the neighbours, like he said he would, remember? Try to trick them into opening their garage? And if they got uptight or defensive about opening the garage..."

"...that'd be a clue that they might be guilty and it'd help to get the magistrate to sign the search warrant. Yes, I remember!" said Rebecca, testily.

"Exactly! Well, they *did* get uptight and didn't allow the police into the garage, but the magistrate *still* said it wasn't enough to justify the search warrant! They need some hard evidence and they just don't have it!"

That evening, Rebecca started rummaging through her tall wardrobe. Within two or three minutes she had her bed covered with clothes. Jasmine watched Rebecca curiously as she started sorting them into groups of trousers and tops, or skirts and blouses. Then she began colour-matching them.

"Wha' are you doing?"

Rebecca answered without looking up.

"Choosing clothes for tomorrow morning."

"For whatsisname? Rayburne?" asked Jasmine, her eyebrows rising up her forehead.

"Well, yeah. Why?"

"He's not your boyfriend, y'know."

"I know." Rebecca put down a pair of jeans and turned to face Jasmine, with her own eyebrows raised, questioningly.

"So," continued Jasmine, "why are you taking so long to choose your clothes?"

"Well…it's just that…I thought I should try to make a good impression on him," said Rebecca. "He might be more willing to talk to us…"

Jasmine cut her off.

"He's already 'willing to talk to us', dumbo! He was the one who arranged the meeting!"

Dropping a T-shirt onto the bed, Rebecca crossed the room and slouched next to Jasmine.

"You're right, but I want him to treat us seriously. I don't know what he's going to say, but it could be really important. I really want to help Ida. She's suffered for such a long time – 35 years, Jaz! That's almost three times as long as we've been alive!"

"All right, I get it. I'll help you choose your clothes. An' you can help me…not that I've got much to choose from," Jasmine said, grinning. "All my stuff's at 'ome!"

Later that night, Rebecca lay awake in bed, going through the last few day's events: the new, creepy neighbours moving in across the road; the accident to her Aunt that had thrown Jasmine and herself together; the Rottweiler chasing her across the road; the revelations about Ida's husband; the kidnapping of Jasmine's friend, Alice; the police visits; the Rayburnes… it all whirled through her head as she tried to make some sense of how her life had been turned upside down…and it hadn't even been a week!

Her mind drifted as unconsciousness began to overtake her…suddenly she sat up. Something had woken her. She wasn't sure what, but something…A noise…from downstairs.

But everyone was in bed!

"Jaz," hissed Rebecca. "JAZ!"

"Wha-whus wrong?" Jasmine's bleary-eyed expression was barely visible in the dark. Rebecca picked her way rapidly across the room in the dark, avoiding Jasmine's belongings by memory, now.

"There's someone downstairs...I think someone's breaking in! I'm going to get Dad." Now completely awake, Jasmine followed her. Creeping across the landing, the girls saw torch beams zigzagging from the kitchen over the wooden flooring and photographs in the hall.

Rebecca quietly entered her parents' bedroom and shook her father awake but covered his mouth immediately. She whispered the situation hastily in his ear.

"Phone the police," he whispered to Sarah as he headed for the bedroom door. "And keep the girls here. I'm going downst..."

"Not without this..." Sarah Roberts threw him one of the two baseball bats she always kept by her bed, "...or me! No thief is going to steal from us and no one's going to hurt my family!" Terry Roberts caught the bat one-handed and smiled, grimly. There was no argument – you never argued with Sarah Roberts when she was in that mood.

"Rebecca. Police!" His whisper was audible from the other side of the room. "Jasmine. Stay with your brother and sister." Then he and his wife slipped quietly out of the room.

The response from the police switchboard was rapid.

"Please help us," said Rebecca in her loudest whisper. "There're thieves in our house!"

"What's your name and address, please?"

"Rebecca Roberts, 4, Pine Tree Close, Colbourne Village, CO18 3DD."

"We'll send a squad car. It should be with you very soon," said the calm voice on the other end of the phone line. Meanwhile, Rebecca had sneaked over to the door, opened it a crack and peeked breathlessly from her vantage point into the hall. Her parents were tiptoeing into the family room.

"Please hurry. My Mum and Dad have just gone downstairs to…"

Smashing glass and a loud yell stopped Rebecca from finishing her sentence. She froze! There was a moment's silence.

"Miss, what's going on? Miss?"

"Shh!" Rebecca silenced her as she strained to hear what was happening. It was just six metres away but it might as well have been six kilometres. Raised voices could be heard.

"Miss!"

"Be quiet!"

She could pick out her Mum's voice, then her Dad's… then…a deep voice that sounded familiar. The argument raged back and forth, yet Rebecca couldn't pick out more than the odd word. She hardly dared breathe.

Then there was a roar followed by shouts, crashing furniture, grunts and groans.

"AAHH!"

"NOOO!"

Rebecca dropped the phone, sailed over the banister and onto the upper landing. She took the last eight stairs in two strides and flew towards the family room. She halted at the door and took in everything in a millisecond.

At either side of the window at the far end of the room, two figures stood: the shorter, older one, grimacing as he held the left side of his head and breathing hard, a sledgehammer in his hand; the other, much taller – also panting – was holding a crowbar, but looked unhurt.

Immediately in front of her, Sarah Roberts was supporting her husband's bloodied head in her lap.

Life slapped Rebecca in the face.

It was her mother's voice.

"Call an ambulance! Rebecca! CALL AN AMBULANCE!"

She staggered, dazed, out of the room into the kitchen and picked up the phone from the breakfast bar. As she tapped in '999', she realised that she was not alone. She turned her head slowly. The large face of a Rottweiler, saliva dripping from its jaws, produced a deep growl from the open, outside door of the kitchen.

"Emergency services. Which service do you require?" inquired a voice on the phone.

Staring directly into the dog's eyes, Rebecca forced herself to stay calm.

"Ambulance." Within seconds she relayed the essential information that could help save her father's life to the operator and disconnected, all the while, never removing her eyes from the dog's. If she looked away, even for a moment, the dog would attack. She felt it; she knew it; she expected it.

"Girl…" came a deep voice.

Rebecca looked away.

The dog leapt forward, its jaws wide.

A shocked rottweiler hung in the air, mid-leap – its teeth, centimetres from her neck. The surprise on its face was almost comical.

Almost.

"Mmmm!" The 'creature' from across the road was holding the huge dog in one arm. She could see him clearly for the first time: pitch black, emotionless eyes, sat below a broad forehead with wild, black eyebrows and even wilder black hair. The pale skin was pockmarked and scarred, while the thin lips uncovered yellowing, uneven teeth that were spread like old tombstones above a massive, darkly bristled jaw. His weathered, floor-length, leather jacket failed to hide the enormous physique that held the huge dog so effortlessly.

"Girl!" The voice again – the same one she'd heard the other night. The same one that had sent Satan after her. She turned her head slowly to her left. In contrast to the 'creature', he was much smaller, with a shaved head and designer stubble. His long face had equally dark, but angry, flashing eyes, that looked straight into Rebecca. The bags under the eyes, the dark swelling over his left temple, the drawn cheeks and the scars that crossed his broad mouth and chin, added to the impression that this was a man who lived by violence.

"Girl…stay out of our way…and keep the police out of our way, too. Or what happened in there…" he jerked his head towards the family room, "…could happen to you, your mother…and the other kids. You got a nice, comfortable life, here," he said, looking around the room with a humourless grin. "Everything's been real easy for you, hasn't it? Hah! It's not like that for everyone, girl. Some of us have to fight to live. Now, you want to keep your nice, easy life, with your nice, easy family? Then keep out of our business. And keep your mouth shut about tonight! Don't talk to the police! Get it?"

Rebecca watched, motionless, as they left. Five minutes later, the police arrived. Ten minutes after that, the ambulance carried her father's unconscious body to the hospital.

THURSDAY

It was 7am.

It was already 20 degrees Celsius outside.

Inside, the living room felt cold.

At least, it did to Rebecca.

Dark shadows hung under her eyes as she tried to take in what had happened in the last seven hours.

She remembered her Mum holding her Dad in her arms before the police arrived, pleading with Rebecca to stay quiet about who had attacked them.

"They meant what they said, Rebecca. On my own I can't protect you. And I don't want you and your cousins to get hurt like...like your..." an array of emotions had crossed Sarah Roberts' face as she had struggled to control her voice. "...like your Father."

She remembered Sergeant Smith and PC Sharma with their sympathy and then their frustration when she couldn't – wouldn't – answer their questions.

She remembered the medics: their kindness, gentleness and rapid, efficient work on her father, stemming the bleeding and quickly getting him into the ambulance.

She remembered the short ride to the local hospital with Jamie and Emily in their pyjamas, cuddling up between her and Jasmine. She remembered the antiseptic, uncaring corridors and the hard, uncomfortable chairs in the waiting room.

She remembered the surgeon, removing his mask as he approached her Mum, their whispered conversation and her Mum hugging him: Terry Roberts was alive and stable, but unconscious.

She remembered her Mum phoning Uncle Gary and the anger in her voice when he had refused to take his children because of 'work commitments'.

"He'll come later this afternoon," Sarah Roberts had told her, between gritted teeth, "just before he picks up Aunt Leanne with her bruised bum!" On any other occasion, Rebecca would have laughed.

She remembered Sarah Roberts bringing them home, cooking them a big breakfast, instructing her and Jasmine to look after Jamie and Emily and keep the front door tightly locked. She remembered the 24-hour locksmith putting a new, powerful lock on the kitchen door, just before her Mum returned to the hospital.

"Becks?" Jasmine stood in the doorway, her brow furrowed. "You OK?"

"What do you think?"

"What can I do, Becks?"

"You can help me to…I wish you *could* help me to… to…those…those…GAARGH! If we were older and stronger…I'd like to…I want to…" Rebecca's hands were white, balled fists, trembling in her lap. Her eyes were flame. It frightened Jasmine to see her cousin like this.

"I know what you're going through, Becks and I'm sorry…"

"How can you know? No one knows!" The sharpness of her reply made Jasmine start. But she didn't react. She knew Rebecca's anger was not aimed at her. She crossed the room, crouched down beside her and laid a hand lightly on one of the rock-like fists.

"You can't fight them with these. You need to use this," Jasmine said, tapping her temple. "Talk to the police: tell them what happened."

"Mum won't let me. She's scared for us. Scared that they'll hurt us," said Rebecca.

"We'll be fine. Just…"

"NO!" shouted Rebecca. "I won't go against her on this. We've got to keep the kids safe."

"Okay," said Jasmine gently, "we'll do that."

"But…I've still got a job to do. I promised. I've got to meet Mr Rayburne."

"But your Dad…"

"I can't help him! Just like you can't help Alice. Mum's with him. I've got to do something to *stop* thinking about him or I'm gonna go *mad*, Jaz!" She raked her fingers through her hair. "I keep seeing his face covered in blood. I've never seen him look weak or helpless, before! He's always been strong." Her head dropped into her hands. "Jaz…I've got to meet Mr Rayburne at 10 o'clock. If I can't help Dad, I can still try to help Ida." She looked imploringly at Jasmine. "One of us has to see him. Can you keep an eye on your brother and sister while I go?"

"Sure," whispered Jasmine as she hugged her cousin, tenderly.

A few hours later, Rebecca was standing, impatiently, outside the coffee shop. It was 10.15. No sign of him. Where was he?

Looking up and down the shopping mall with its shiny, stone tiles, windows patterned with adverts for the latest mobile phones from the phone stores, and the brightly lit shops full of people of all ages, happily bustling around with logo-covered bags; none of them knew how she was feeling. None of them had just had their worlds decimated. None of them felt the weight of responsibility that was crushing her young shoulders. None of them saw the world in cold shades of grey like she did. How could they be so happy?

Driving the thoughts from her mind, Rebecca tried to focus on finishing what she had started. Nothing – and no one – would stop her. She was determined.

"Hello Miss…Miss…"

A familiar pair of piercing blue eyes below a mane of silver hair, studied her, intently. It was Mr Rayburne.

"Roberts. Rebecca Roberts. Call me Rebecca." She tried to smile, but it felt more like a grimace.

"OK, Rebecca. Please, call me David. Your friend isn't with you?"

"My frie…? Oh, you mean my cousin. No, she has to babysit her brother and sister."

"I see. Uh, you look rather pale. Are you all right?" he asked.

"I-I didn't sleep very well, that's all," said Rebecca, quickly. "Let's go in."

They entered the coffee shop and David Rayburne bought a latte for himself and an ice-cream coffee for Rebecca. They found a table in the corner of the shop where they could talk, undisturbed. David Rayburne sat with his back to the other customers at the metallic, ebony table, thoughtfully stirring his latte, as if – Rebecca thought – he was searching for the right words to say. She, in turn, played with the whipped cream in her cup till he was ready. At last he spoke.

"I'm...I'm sorry you had to go through that yesterday. But the shock of your questions...and the memories it brought back were so...so *raw*, that her feelings just...overwhelmed her," Rebecca stopped playing with her cream, her face reddening with guilt. "You see, she hasn't been well...for a very long time. Ever since..." He paused, his lips struggling to form words while at the same time his eyebrows twitched. After a minute of uncomfortable silence, he continued: "Thirty-five years ago, we were a very happy family. Julie and I were childhood sweethearts. A lovelier, sweeter girl you couldn't hope to meet. Full of energy and life..."

Rebecca thought of the woman she had met the day before. It seemed impossible he was talking about the same person. She tuned back in to what he was saying.

"...the day she told me she was pregnant, oh, her eyes were dancing! You know, she was a fantastic mother. Our daughter, Katie, loved her and Julie was brilliant at guiding her through all her childhood problems, helping her with her work and teaching her how to be really kind and caring. Even when she was very young, you could see what an influence Julie'd had on her. She was such a sweet and gentle child...

"Then...then *it* happened." The piercing blue eyes had dimmed. His voice was hoarse. "We did everything we could to find Katie: we searched everywhere; we went on TV to beg the kidnapper to return her; we put pleas in the newspapers...but nothing worked.

"That's when Julie changed. At first, she felt it was all her fault, letting Katie go out on her own. But how was she to know? She'd done the same thing so many times and our village was so safe. How *could* she know?" He sighed deeply. "Then she turned on me: *I* should've been there to pick Katie up; *I* should've been a better dad; *I* should've looked after my family more carefully; *I* didn't care enough…and so it went on, day after day. This wonderful wife and mother…the hate and venom just poured out on anyone who was close to her."

"Like Ida's husband, Shahin?" interjected Rebecca. His tear-wet eyes dropped, unable to bear what he might see in Rebecca's face when next he spoke.

"Yes. He did so much to help us find Katie. But the police took him in for questioning – some anonymous tip-off, apparently, that he'd offered her a lift that awful afternoon. She would have gone with him, too, because she loved him. We *all* loved Shahin and Ida. They were our best friends. And they really loved Katie. I knew that. I *always* knew that. But…but after the police took him away, Julie…just tore into them. Once she started, she couldn't stop. The papers fanned the flames, because…"

"…they said he was a terrorist or something, because he came from Iran? Yeah. Ida told me," said Rebecca. "But you said yesterday that you knew he wasn't guilty."

"Yes. Yes." David Rayburne went silent for a moment. "You see, she was filled with so much rage that when I tried – and I did try, really I did – when I tried to make her see reason, that there was no way Ida and Shahin could have hurt her, she rounded on me again. Why wasn't I backing her up? Why was I attacking her? Did I think it was her fault Katie was gone? No matter what I said it was turned against me, until I couldn't fight her any more.

"Anyway, one day I ran into Shahin and...I had a go at him. I said dreadful things...awful, unspeakable things about him and what he'd done...lies, just so I could prove to Julie that I was on her side."

Mr Rayburne was visibly shaking: tears began to drip down his cheeks. A couple of middle-aged ladies behind him turned around to see what was going on. Rebecca ignored them. Conflicted with both fury at – and compassion for – the Rayburnes, she compelled herself to rest her hand on his forearm and gently squeeze it.

"Go on," she whispered.

Wiping his eyes with the back of his hand, he managed to regain his composure.

"I never saw him again. And then, a few months later, we heard he'd died. Julie sort of smiled when she got the news. But I couldn't. I couldn't. I kept remembering the last words I'd said to him, Rebecca. If you'd seen him that day – I saw his heart break in front of me. What I did...what I did was kill him! Just used words as weapons instead of my hands. I can't forgive myself. Ever."

Silence again.

Now, after what she had just heard, it was Rebecca who struggled to speak.

"What–what made you tell me?"

"What made me..?" Mr Rayburne looked almost surprised. Then an expression of comprehension crossed his face. "Of course, of course. How could you *possibly* know?"

He put his hand into the small chest pocket of his light-blue, denim shirt. From it he pulled a smaller, square piece of what looked like coloured paper on one side and white on the other. He looked at it. His eyes moistened once more. Then he turned it round to face Rebecca. She squinted at it for a moment, then her eyes widened.

"Because of her," breathed Rebecca.

"Because of you," he replied.

Rebecca was staring at a photograph of a young girl, no more than nine or ten, with dark hair and green eyes.

"She looks like me!"

"Yes. I nearly died when I saw your face, yesterday. You look so much like my Katie...Catherine...would have done at your age."

"Well...how come Mrs Rayburne didn't notice that?" asked Rebecca.

"Julie's never got past Katie's disappearance," said Mr Rayburne, "so she can't imagine her a day older than she was then. But I've often wondered how she'd look as she grew up."

"I see," said Rebecca. Then she frowned. "But... you've got blue eyes and Mrs Rayburne has brown. How come Katie...?"

"Her grandmother. The most beautiful green eyes you've ever seen. Just like yours." His smile was warmer this time. In return, a small smile broke across Rebecca's tired, young face.

"I've got to go now, Rebecca. Maybe you could tell Ida how truly sorry I am for what I did." He got up to leave; Rebecca grabbed his hand.

"Why don't you tell her yourself?"

"No, I couldn't face her after how I treated Shahin," he replied.

"She might surprise you," pleaded Rebecca. But he shook his head.

"Please don't ask it of me."

Rebecca decided not to press the point. Mr Rayburne turned to leave.

"Oh, what about your photograph?" She thrust it towards him. He raised a gentle hand in objection.

"No. No, I'd like you to have it. I brought it for you. I have another copy at home. Please keep it."

She nodded as she brought her hand – and the photograph – back. He smiled again, then gently leant forward and kissed her on the brow of her head. The middle-aged ladies nudged each other.

"Bye, Katie dear," he said. Then he left without looking back.

Rebecca sat down again and gazed at the photograph. Green eyes. Dark hair. She shook her head. They looked so much alike, although Rebecca never felt comfortable wearing jewellery; whereas Katie had a gold necklace with the letter 'C' in the middle of flat, diagonal links…

"Why 'C'?" she said to herself. "Her name was Katie. Ohh…of course, that's short for 'Catherine'. That explains…Hold on: did he just call *me* Katie?" She thought for a moment and sat up straight. "Did he just kiss me on top of my head?"

All through her half hour journey home, Rebecca tried to formulate a plan that could help clear Shahin's name and find Jasmine's friend, Alice. But her mind was so full of worry for her Dad and she was so tired, that her thoughts were racing through her brain at the speed of glue. She had to sleep, clear her mind and then put a strategy together.

When she unlocked the door, the house was quiet. The kitchen, living room and dining room were all empty. She crept up the stairs and gently pushed open the bedroom door to Jamie's and Emily's room. Both were in a deep sleep. Jamie's duvet was all askew. One of his arms overhung the edge of the mattress, while his tousled, fair-haired head had burrowed into his pillow and some drool dripped on to the bed sheet from his open mouth.

Emily had pulled her duvet over her head, so nothing of her face was visible. But Rebecca could just make out the rhythmic rising and falling of the bedcovers. Funny how the little horrors were so quiet and angelic when they were asleep.

Avoiding the creaking floorboard just outside the door of her own room, she slowly depressed the door handle. Jasmine's familiar, quiet snoring, so irritating a few days ago, was now quite comforting.

She silently undressed and slipped into her T-shirt and shorts. Then she crawled into bed, the sheets and thin, summer duvet feeling cool and comfortable against her bare arms, neck and legs. This time her mind did not drift. She was asleep in seconds. But it was not the restful sleep she had been hoping for.

Rebecca was interested in dreams and had once carried out some research for a school project. Scientific experiments had shown that people dream about six times a night: in the first few dreams, the mind tries to work out problems encountered during the day. What the scientists would have made of Rebecca's dreams – the miasma of violent images, tears, arguments, threats, confessions, chases and kidnapping – is anyone's guess. Were any problems solved? Not that Rebecca could tell.

Part of the dream kept repeating, beginning with Mr Rayburne and Mrs Rayburne, Ida and Shahin, yelling at each other. Suddenly, Katie appeared pleading with them to stop; then the adults started pulling her this way and that way, by her arms, her hair and, finally, her neck! Someone grabbed her gold neck chain and it tightened round her throat, as Katie scrabbled and scratched at it.

Gradually, Katie transformed into Rebecca, or rather, Rebecca became Katie. She saw and felt what Katie saw and felt: angry adults' contorted faces, their hands grasping and tearing at her; the pain round her throat growing in intensity and her gasping for breath that came through straining lungs and shallow, searing breaths. She struggled to break the chain, but the more she struggled, the tighter it became.

Finally, she woke up, her heart beating wildly, cold sweat on her back and angry faces burning in her memory. Why were they trying to kill her? What had she done wrong? When would they try again?

It took her several minutes to convince herself that it *was* a dream: no one had tried to kill her. A dream... only a dream...but why did it repeat? Why was it so important? What was it trying to tell her? But the details simply slipped from her mind like liquid metal through the holes in a sieve. Scientists would have politely explained that dreams leave the weakest memory traces, so it's normal to forget them. Rebecca would have politely explained how unhelpful that explanation was to her, at that moment – perhaps not so politely!

She sat up and surveyed the room. Jasmine was no longer there. She jumped out of bed, dashed out of the room and checked the other bedroom. Empty. Dimly, she heard noise rising up the stairs. The sounds suggested that all three of them were in the kitchen. And from the warm, savoury smells accompanying their hubbub, a late lunch was being cooked. Mmmm...she felt hungry for the first time since the previous evening. Then her stomach tightened. Did they know how to cook? What condition would the kitchen be in?

Flames and smoke pouring from the cooker, tomato ketchup-smeared, smashed plates littering the floor... she shuddered at the idea.

Mum'll go mad, she thought.

Rushing downstairs, she almost overshot the kitchen door in her haste. When she peeked round the doorway, however, she was agog.

Jasmine was at the cooker, frying bacon and eggs like a professional chef, while Emily and Jamie were putting out the plates, knives, forks and ketchup at Jasmine's instruction. She was like a conductor directing an obedient orchestra. Rebecca marvelled at the sight. Never had she seen them working as a team.

"Hey guys. I'm impressed! Is there enough of that food to go round? I'm starving!" Jamie and Emily grinned at her.

"There's lotsa food!" Jamie exclaimed.

"Yeah! An' Jaz is good at bacon 'n' eggs!" chimed in Emily.

Jasmine gave an embarrassed grin.

"Yeah, well, I've had lots of practice. Dad can't cook and Mum got me doing fry-ups a long time ago, 'cos she goes out to work before we get up. Come on, Becks. Sit down and eat your breakfast...uh...lunch...uh... wha'ever!!"

Rebecca beamed as she strode in and leapt into the nearest chair. She gobbled up the food and even had second helpings, with four slices of heavily buttered toast – the last one with thick strawberry jam on top – much to Jasmine's surprise and delight.

"Where'd you get an appetite like that, Becks?"

Rebecca thought for a moment.

"Ebay," she said, straight-faced.

The two girls stared at each other, smiles twitching at the corner of their mouths. Suddenly, they collapsed in a fit of giggles; Emily and Jamie just looked bemused.

"What're they laughing at?" asked Jamie.

"They're teenagers, innit?" replied Emily, while the two girls laughed, helplessly.

"Oh! Oh! I shouldn't laugh!" groaned a creased-up Rebecca, tears running down her face. "My stomach's so full it hurts!!".

"That'll–that'll teach you!" Jasmine replied breathlessly, holding her sides. "Ow! Now *I've* got a stitch!"

That set Rebecca off again and for five minutes they alternated between hysterical laughter and groans of indigestion. Emily shook her head at the two of them, then turned to her brother, crossed her eyes, pointed to her head and rotated her index finger. Jamie chewed his toast, nodding, knowingly.

"Brrriiing! Brrriiing!"

Rebecca staggered over to the phone, clutching her stomach.

"He–hello?" she said, trying desperately to control herself. In a moment she was calm. "I'll be right there." She turned to see the quizzical expression on her cousin's tear-stained features. "It's Ida."

Moments after changing back into her day clothes, she was banging on Ida's front door.

"That you, Becca, love?"

"Yes, Ida. Open up."

Behind the door, Rebecca heard a lock, a bolt and a chain being unlocked, drawn back and unhooked, one after the other. Rebecca was surprised – Ida was always up early in the morning and it was now after 2pm. Why hadn't she unlocked the door till now? The door opened, hesitantly. Ida's anxious face peered through the opening. Then the door opened wide.

"Come in quick!" Ida's bony fingers grabbed Rebecca's slender, elegant hand and pulled her through the doorway. Ida had a final, quick look outside and then slammed and bolted the door once more. Rebecca could not understand her strange behaviour. She opened her mouth to say something, but Ida ushered her into the living room and pointed at the chair for her to sit down. When they were both seated, Rebecca noticed she was very pale.

"What's going on, Ida? You look scared."

"Why'd you have to get involved, Becca? It wasn't your job to do that!"

Rebecca was taken aback.

"Wha–what d'you mean? It wasn't my job? To do what?"

"It's more than thirty years ago, Becca. It's the past. I didn't want people dragging it up again!" Ida's hands were trembling and Rebecca guessed why.

"You're my friend, Ida. I just wanted to help…"

"It 'asn't!" Ida shouted back. "It's made things worse. Much worse. I didn't want to see her again… least ways, not like that."

"Who, Ida? Who are you talking about?"

"She came banging on my door this morning. I thought it was the postman with a package or something, but it was 'er."

"Ida...who came 'banging on your door'?"

"Julie Rayburne!"

"Mrs Rayburne?" Now it was Rebecca who turned pale. "What did she say?"

"Dreadful things, Becca. Terrible things. She pushed her way into the house and started screaming at me. She wanted to know how I had the nerve to send you snooping round. She said it was Katie who was the victim, not Shahin! The things she said about him. I can't bear to think about it. But the look on 'er face; I've never seen so much hate. She said she wouldn't let me get away with it. She said she'd drag Shahin's name through the dirt again and make sure the newspapers would hound me for the rest of my days. She said she'd get her solicitor on to me 'cos I sent you to cause her distress. Becca, she never stopped screaming at me. It was horrible...horrible!"

She broke down. Rebecca rushed across and put her arm around her. For the first time she realised just how frail she was: Rebecca felt Ida's shoulder bones trembling beneath her hands as Ida sobbed. Rebecca was too scared to hug her tightly, in case she hurt her.

"I'm really sorry, Ida. I only wanted to help. I...I just wanted to find out what really happened so I could prove that Shahin was innocent, once and for all. I thought maybe they had some information that might help. It didn't occur to me that..."

"That it might stir up bad memories or get people angry and upset?" Ida's expression was harsh for a moment, but Rebecca's downcast demeanour quickly softened her. "Nah, I s'pose you didn't. You're young and think you can solve all the world's problems. I thought the same when I was your age. You think you can take on the world and win." She squeezed Rebecca's hand. "Thanks for what you've tried to do, love. I do appreciate it, really. I don't think we'll get any answers now, though. Not after all these years."

Rebecca knew she was probably right, but she couldn't give up so easily. She stayed with Ida for another half an hour to make sure she was okay and they chatted about everything: the news, the weather, the economy. Rebecca decided not to burden Ida with news about her Dad and the threats from the new neighbours: she was delicate enough without the extra pressure of Rebecca's problems.

When she got back home, Rebecca could hear muffled shouting from upstairs. What on earth was going on? Had Jamie been discovered putting worms in odd places? Had Emily finally been found stealing from her? Rebecca took the stairs two at a time. By the time she reached her bedroom door, the shouting had become yelling. Cautiously, she entered her bedroom.

Jasmine was pacing the room, crimson-faced, one hand by her left cheek, her voice reaching new levels of decibel power. For a moment Rebecca thought she must be losing it; then she realised Jasmine was on her smart phone.

"You don't care, you just don't care! You say you do, but you don't! I hate you! I never want to see you again!"

Rebecca stood for a moment, open-mouthed as Jasmine disconnected her call with a stab of her finger and continued her tirade while she wore a furrow into the carpet, hot tears pouring down her reddened cheeks.

"Mean...uncaring...hate that..." Then she stopped, mid-stride, turning her gaze towards Rebecca. "How long have you been standing there?" she demanded, her eyes glinting, fiercely.

"Not long," Rebecca replied, a little nervously. "What's going on, Jaz?"

"Dad."

"What about him?"

"He's not going to pick us up!"

"Why?"

"He reckons Mum needs time to get used to being back at home without us. We'd be rushing around her and getting under her feet when she's trying to get back on hers. She might have another fall...he says! He's such a liar! He just wants peace and quiet. Kids only get in his way. I HATE him!"

Rebecca looked down, embarrassed and annoyed for her cousin. She felt Jasmine's anger: Uncle Gary liked having a family, but not the hard work that went with it.

Then, the main door downstairs slammed.

"REBECCA!"

"Mum!" Grabbing Jasmine's hand, Rebecca dashed out of the door and down the stairs. Racing into the kitchen, they found Sarah Roberts rubbing her eyes.

"Mum?" Rebecca asked, more warily this time. Sarah Roberts' eyes were bloodshot and all round her eyes she was red and puffy and her cheeks were wet. Rebecca 's blood froze. "Mum...wha-what's happened?"

Her mother looked up.

"It's your Dad."

The antiseptic atmosphere of the hospital hadn't changed. They trudged the endless corridors till they reached Banbury Ward. Sarah Roberts and the four children entered the private room to the right of the ward entrance, quietly, as if afraid of waking the dead. Rebecca approached the bed, cautiously. Terry Roberts lay on the bed, pale and motionless. Rebecca slowly reached out her hand and softly touched her father's arm. Her eyes began to well up.

"D-Dad," she said, gently.

"Mmm…" Unfocused eyes flickered open and peered around the room for several seconds, trying to achieve clarity. "Hello love." Terry Roberts' voice crackled like dry, autumn leaves. His fingers gently brushed a tear from his daughter's cheek. "I'm all right."

"I know," she replied. "Mum told us. Just happy to see you awake." She bit her lip as the image of her helpless, bleeding father, flashed into her mind. Sarah Roberts stood behind them, her arms around Jasmine – who was also crying – and Jamie and Emily, who were grinning from ear to ear.

"Why are you wearing a silly, white hat?" shouted Jamie. Rebecca laughed, in spite of herself.

"It's a bandage, dingbat!" said Jasmine nudging her little brother. After the laughter subsided, Terry Roberts said:

"Jaz. Can you do me a favour?"

"Sure, Uncle Terry," Jasmine smiled, glad to feel useful.

"Can you go and get the kids a snack from the shop down the corridor? "Sarah, love, give her some cash will you?" Sarah Roberts looked quizzically at her husband, but pulled out a handful of pound coins anyway and handed them to Jasmine. Just before closing the door behind them, Rebecca gave her arm a friendly squeeze. Jasmine returned her a lop-sided smile and ushered the children out. "Sarah, we need to talk and I wanted Rebecca in here, 'cos this is a family, decision."

"Decision?" Sarah Roberts was confused. "What are you talking about? What decision?"

"Since I woke up, I've been thinking hard about what happened…in between the headaches. I know you were talking to me when you thought I couldn't hear you last night. I guess I was semi-conscious or something; I heard every word you said, though I can't remember all of it. And I understand why you made a decision like you did; but it's got to change."

"You don't mean…" Sarah Roberts began.

"That's exactly what I do mean."

"No, we can't. I told you why. It's not safe. I can't allow it."

"We've got no choice, Sarah! We can't let it stand!"

"Don't tell me what we can and can't do! *You're* in here! *I'm* the one who has to…"

"Will somebody please tell me what you're arguing about?" Rebecca cut in, worried and exasperated at the way the disagreement was getting louder and angrier.

"Your father wants to tell the police what happened!" Sarah Roberts fumed as she turned to her daughter. "I told you I can't keep you and the children safe by myself. You do understand, don't you, Rebecca?"

"Sarah," said Terry Roberts, "we can't let these people get away with it. If they think they can do this now, the whole neighbourhood will be under their reign of terror. Heaven knows what they'll be capable of if we don't stand up to them, now. Right now!"

Rebecca had never before heard her father speak with such passion. Her eyes flicked back and forth between her parents as they pleaded their cases. They meant every word they said. They knew they were right. They loved each other. They loved her. She hesitated; she knew she would have to disappoint one of them and she knew which one it was. She took a deep breath before she spoke.

"Mum...Dad...a week ago...all my worries were about homework, Tae Kwon Do lessons and Aunt Leanne and Uncle Gary coming to visit – don't look at me like that Dad. I don't like them and I never have! I can't help that. But a lot has happened this week. I've been chased by a Rottweiler, interviewed by the police, threatened by a thug..." she paused for breath and to collect her thoughts. There was so much to say. "...I've cried for Ida's dead husband, cos he was accused of a crime he didn't commit. I've cried for Jasmine 'cos her Dad makes her feel she's not good enough and 'cos she's lost her best friend. I've cried with Mum because *you* were...attacked... Dad and 'cos I thought I'd lost you for good. But I've learned that I can't just cry. I've got to do some things for myself and no one can do them for me.

"So, I'm going to help Ida by proving that her husband, Shahin, didn't do anything wrong; somehow, I'm going to help Jasmine find out what happened to her friend who disappeared a couple of days ago; and...I'm going to help you – and the neighbourhood – by telling the police exactly what happened last night!"

"Just a moment..." her mother began, but Rebecca cut her short.

"We'll get police protection, just like in the movies!"

The conversation ended there. Sarah Roberts knew when she was beaten. "She's not just a kid any more, Sarah," said Terry Roberts smiling proudly at his daughter. "And when I'm better, you can tell me all about your investigations, love. But listen: be sensible. Don't rush into anything. Don't put yourself in danger again. That's how people get hurt." He rubbed his head bandage and gave his daughter a knowing look.

"OK, Dad," Rebecca replied, "I get the message: safety first."

"Good," her father said. Then he squeezed his wife's hand. "Sarah, please take everyone home, now. I'm very tired and I need to rest." They hugged and kissed him in turn, then he closed his eyes and quickly fell asleep.

"So, they told you to…stay out of their way, or…what happened to your Dad would happen to you, your Mum and your cousins, right?" Sgt Smith's jaw seemed even more prominent as he read over PC Sharma's notes and his expression was grim.

"Yes, that's right," Rebecca replied.

"And this was the older, shorter, one?"

Rebecca nodded.

"Mrs Roberts, was he the one who hit your husband?"

"No, that was the bigger man." PC Sharma updated her words rapidly in her notebook. "Thanks for coming to the station to file the complaint, though I really wish you'd told us earlier, Mrs Roberts," continued the officer. Sarah Roberts pursed her lips and nodded slowly, without looking up. "But I can appreciate that you were frightened for your family and it's taken a lot of courage on your part to agree to be witnesses.

"We've taken a statement from your husband, already. He can't remember the actual fight – not unusual after being knocked unconscious – but he does remember them entering the house, illegally. We can now go ahead with a raid on their house. It'll probably be tonight in the early hours. The sooner the better: they won't be expecting it, now. They'll still think you're too scared of them so they won't come around again."

"Thanks. It'll be a weight off my mind," Sarah Roberts smiled, thinly. The strain was etched across her face and Rebecca was shocked when she realised how much older her mother suddenly appeared.

That evening, everything was normal; or as normal as Sarah Roberts could keep it. Jamie and Emily were oblivious to everything except their games or their TV programmes. Jasmine and Rebecca were sombre and helped Mum make the dinner, do the washing up and put the two young ones to bed.

She didn't insist on Rebecca and Jasmine getting to bed at their usual time. She was grateful for their company, but she was filled with conflicting feelings: excitement that the thugs who had hurt her husband would be caught; dread, that the raid could fail and the terrible consequences for her family. She didn't share these thoughts with the girls, but she had the feeling they understood.

Rebecca did all she could to lighten the mood that evening, making lots of jokes that kept her mother giggling.

Jasmine followed suit. Rebecca had been an annoying, selfish, pain in the neck; but now, for Jasmine, she had become something unexpected – a sister. A week ago she would have happily thumped her. Now she would do anything for her. Life was strange.

FRIDAY

After midnight, they went to bed, exhausted. Sarah Roberts – having barely slept in almost two days – was asleep in seconds. Rebecca and Jasmine got changed, without talking, but gave each other a tired smile before putting out the light and falling into a deep sleep.

"One, two, three!" The police rams took out the huge door and locks in three blows. "POLICE! POLICE! This is a raid! Get down on the floor! AAAGH!" The lead officer in riot gear collapsed. The police were confronted by a nightmare of a man, wielding a thirty-kilo steel bar one-handed! Three officers charged him with batons raised. One was floored with an expert stroke, while the other two, dodging the weapon, piled into his legs and torso. He dropped the bar and, ripping the officers off him, threw them around like rag dolls. Outside in the driveway, police dogs were in a vicious fight with Satan and his younger sibling, each trying to get a grip on the other's throat.

By the garage, more officers were in a pitched battle with the brothers, ducking their swinging, spiked chains and fending off powerful machete blows with their batons. The older, scar-faced man, managed to slice his way through the officers and raced out into the street. His eyes, wild, at first, became keenly focused. He strode across the road like a malevolent colossus. The front door of 4, Pine Tree Close, splintered at one, violent blow. He rushed up the stairs, yelling as he came:

"Girl! Where are you, girl?" The bedroom door flew open and he came for Rebecca. There was nowhere to run or hide. He lifted the terrified girl with one hand and began shaking her, harder and harder and harder...

"Becksy!!"

Rebecca sat up, suddenly, in her bed, covered in cold sweat.

"Becksy!!"

It was Emily, shaking her shoulders. Rebecca blinked rapidly, trying to work out what was going on. *Ohh... more dreams*, she thought.

"Becksy!" said Emily urgently.

"What's up?" whispered Rebecca. Jasmine was still asleep.

"We're hungry!"

Rebecca groaned, inwardly. Her digital clock read 06:30.

"Oh, come on!! It's far too early to..." she stopped as she saw the expectant faces of her cousins. They were too young to understand why she was so tired and perhaps it was better that they didn't. "Oh, all right. Come with me and don't make a noise. Mum and Jaz are fast asleep."

"Okay," whispered Emily. They crept out of the room and downstairs to the kitchen. Quickly, Rebecca got them a bowl each of Frosties (their favourite cereal) and made them some toast with Nutella and honey on the same piece of bread. A sweet tooth? Rebecca wondered if they would have any 'sweet teeth' left by the time they grew up!

Once they had finished, Rebecca took their bowls and plates and put them in the sink to be washed later. Then she spoke firmly to them.

"Now you can watch TV and play games in the family room, but you MUST keep the noise down. Mum and Jaz need to sleep, OK?"

They nodded obediently and put on the 'Kids' section on TV and flicked through the cartoons. Rebecca closed the door, trudged upstairs and fell back into bed, glad of the chance to sleep some more.

As she drifted off, the two youngsters avidly watched the end of one cartoon and looked forward to the next. But they'd seen it before and it was boring. They took out the Monopoly and thought about playing with it, but Emily didn't know the rules and Jamie knew even less. Within a few minutes, they were fed up and searching for things to do. Emily pulled back the curtain and looked out.

"Hey, Jamie, it's lovely outside. Let's go and play." The two went to the porch. Emily could just reach the door handle and tried the front door; it was locked. Jamie looked disappointed. "S'alright, Jamie, I know where Aunt Sarah hangs her keys!" She rushed back into the hallway and took the door key from the right-hand drawer of the small hall cupboard. Rapidly, she unlocked the door, replaced the key and the two were outside. It was 7.10 on a beautiful, late spring morning.

"Hey, Jamie! I've got a good idea! Let's get something to scare Jazzy and Becksy when they wake up." Jamie looked up at his sister, suddenly interested.

"Worms?"

"Nahh! You done that ages ago. Something crawly and scary and wiv' lots of legs," said Emily, her eyes gleaming, wickedly.

"Spiders!"

"Spiders is good. But, there was somefing we saw on the telly the uvver day." Emily scratched her head as she struggled to remember. "It's got a big, spiky tail and it stings an' it can kill you."

"Wasps?"

"Nahh, it can't fly. It's got big claws to grab you."

"Oh, oh, I know!" Jamie's face was alight. "Porkypines!"

Emily collapsed on the floor, giggling madly. When she recovered, she sat up and saw a very cross Jamie staring down at her.

"No, Jamie. Porcupines is too big and it looks like a big hedgehog. Bu' you 'elped me remember...It's scorpions!"

"Yeah...scorpipoms! Where are they? I ain't seen 'em here," said Jamie, looking upset.

"Let's go outside. Maybe near the trees on the street." Emily led the charge across the road.

Ten minutes of fruitless searching later.

"Nuffink!" Jamie's face dropped. "No scorpipoms!"

"Hmmm... Let's go to the end of the road. There's gotta be some scorpions there. Them trees is different, too. Come on!" Grabbing Jamie's hand, Emily pulled him down to the far corner of Pine Tree Close, where a combination of ash, silver birch and oak trees let their leaves hang lazily in the warm sunshine, while insects buzzed, crawled and hopped, oblivious of the two tornados heading towards them.

Digging furiously in the long grass between the bases of the trees, the children tore through the roots. Grasshoppers leapt for their lives in all directions; ants fled the clawing fingers, carrying their eggs as they went; the wasps zig-zagged between the flying clods of earth, looking for quieter ways of earning a meal. The children were so engaged in the scorpion hunt, that, at first, they didn't notice the sun's rays gradually disappearing.

Suddenly, Emily shivered.

"Why's it so cold?" she said, sitting up. She noticed Jamie staring at something behind her. She turned around, slowly.

Jasmine's favourite song rang out on her smart phone. Sleepily, she slapped at the phone till it went silent. Then she picked it up and gazed at it, bleary-eyed.

"Mmm...nine o'clock. Need a shower." Jasmine stumbled into the bathroom and turned on the power shower, waiting for the water to warm up.

Sarah Roberts' eyes flickered open as she heard the water being pumped at high pressure. She gazed at the other side of the bed.

Empty.

Smoothing the pillow where Terry Roberts' head usually lay, she pictured his thick, dark hair with grey patches, sticking out at all sorts of odd angles, after a good night's sleep. She smiled at the memory, until the moment the image was replaced with his pale face, and a white bandage covering his hair.

"Must get up now!" she thought, savagely, clearing the image from her mind. Passing the bathroom door,

Jasmine's voice wafted tunefully out of the shower. "Good singer," thought Sarah Roberts, surprised. Pushing open her daughter's bedroom door, she found Rebecca sprawled across the mattress on her stomach, her thin duvet half hanging off the bed. "Come on, lazy. I didn't have time to get the sponge this time!"

"Wha…?" Rebecca raised her head and tried to work out from which direction the voice had come. After several attempts, she caught sight of her Mum's grin.

"Now you're awake, you can go and get Emily and Jamie up."

Rebecca twisted completely around and sat up.

"No need. Did that ages ago," she answered, running her hand through her hair. "Gave them breakfast, too. They'll either be in the family room watching TV and playing games, or in the garden. You know them. They'll be keeping themselves busy. Funny, I've kind of got used to having them around. It'll almost be a shame when they go."

"Ooh, you *have* changed your tune!" replied her mother. "You weren't saying that a week ago!"

"A week? Ha! Seems like years." She mirrored her mother's grin with one of her own.

Sarah Roberts nodded slowly and her smile broadened.

"Well, let's go and get our own breakfast…after 'Adele' finishes in the shower, that is!"

Rebecca quickly changed into jeans and a T-shirt, then started harmonising with Jasmine from outside the bathroom door.

"Oi, Becks!" yelled Jasmine from the shower. "You'll be arrested for animal cruelty! Stop strangling them cats!!"

"Ouch!" shouted Rebecca in mock offense. "Thank you, Simon Cowell!"

Ten minutes later, the three of them were pouring cereal into bowls and toasting bread.

"Where're Jamie and Emily?" asked Jasmine.

"TV room." replied Rebecca. Jasmine got up and headed to the family room. "You can see it's on through the pebble-glass door, Jaz. Probably watching something on CBBC. *And…*" the loudness of the word caught Jasmine's attention, "…I already fed them."

Spinning around in a fluid, balletic movement, Jasmine returned and sat down to her bowl of Honey Nut Flakes.

"I'm going to see your Dad this morning, before I meet up with one of my clients to go through their accounts," said Rebecca's mother, "so you two keep an eye on Jamie and Emily. And can you please do some vacuuming round here? It's been too long since I've had a chance to do any."

"What time's *my* Dad picking us up, today, Aunt Sarah?"

"Later this afternoon, I think…he was a bit vague…" her voice trailed off as she saw Jasmine's expression.

Rebecca tried to change the subject: "Wonder when we'll find out how the police raid w…" The doorbell interrupted her. Her mother looked out of the kitchen window, then back at her daughter, then out of the window again.

"Are you getting psychic powers or something, Rebecca?" she asked with a laugh. Jasmine and Rebecca stared at each other, quizzically as Sarah Roberts strode out to the back door. Into the room walked Sergeant Smith and PC Sharma. The girls stared at them, laughed out loud, then had to apologise, profusely, to the police officers, whose expressions would have made the front-page picture of a national newspaper!

"Well," said Sergeant Smith, somewhat bemused, "it's good to see smiles on your faces, anyway. PC Sharma, would you like to explain why we're here?" Everyone's focus shifted to the young officer, who was momentarily taken aback.

"Yes, Sarge. Uh...well, the raid went ahead at 4am. The squad of ten officers armed with helmets, shields and light weapons, broke down the door – which wasn't easy as the occupants had installed so many locks! By the time the door came down, the suspects were armed and ready with weapons and Rottweilers. We were expecting the dogs, so we shot them..." The girls looked shocked, but PC Sharma quickly added, "...with a tranquilliser dart! Quite harmless and they'll wake up, soon, in the dog pound. The suspects put up more of a fight, though. Pity we couldn't use the tranquilliser dart on them, eh Sarge?" she grinned, glancing up at her senior colleague. He raised an eyebrow in disapproval. Her grin vanished. "The assault team were well-protected and managed to subdue them. But it did take four of them to take down the big one..."

"The creature," Rebecca muttered to Jasmine.

"The what?" PC Sharma queried.

"Oh, um, it's my nickname for that huge...thing!"

"Oh, okay." PC Sharma continued her narrative. "We arrested the suspects in the house and took them down to the station where they are being questioned."

"However," continued Sergeant Smith, "the suspect you identified as the older man wasn't caught. A vehicle was missing so we think he was away from the house when it was raided."

Sarah Roberts blanched.

"You mean he's still on the loose?"

"I'm afraid so. But don't worry. We've a PC on duty outside your house for security, and he can get help very quickly in any emergency. You'll all be quite safe. In any case, we still have a forensic team and a couple of PCs at their house, looking for any sign of children having been kept there against their will, and if there is evidence, it may point to where they've been taken."

"So, do you think it's safe for me to visit my husband at the hospital?" asked Sarah Roberts, anxiously chewing her lower lip.

"Yes, that's fine, Mrs Roberts. The children will be safe, but," he said, making eye contact with Rebecca and Jasmine, "you two mustn't leave the house." Sarah Roberts looked relieved.

"Well, we'll be on our way, Mrs Roberts. Girls," said Sergeant Smith, giving each of them a reassuring smile. "We'll be in touch to give you updates as and when we have them. Okay?" Then he and PC Sharma headed back to their squad car.

"Thank goodness for that," said Sarah Roberts, hugging the two girls. "They've caught most of them and they'll probably get the leader of the gang, soon. I'm off to see your Dad, now, Rebecca, so go and get a shower. Remember, it's up to you two to look after Jamie and Emily. I'll be back early in the afternoon and we'll have lunch together. Fish and chips?"

"Yes please!" said Jasmine, enthusiastically.

"Rebecca. Shower. Now!"

"OK, Mum, I'm going, I'm going!" She kissed her mother on the cheek and made her promise to give a big kiss to her father.

Two minutes later she was under the hot shower, soaking up the warmth at the back of her neck, wondering what they could do for the rest of the day.

She and Jasmine couldn't go out anywhere so they couldn't do any more investigation for Ida. Emily and Jamie would be more of a problem – they couldn't go to the park, now, to use up some of their energy. But Uncle Gary would be back some time in the afternoon so that would be one less problem to think about.

Mum would take her to see Dad tonight. That'd be good. But there was a nagging worry.

The leader of the gang. What would he do when he saw the police car outside his house? Would he try to sneak back in when it was dark, or would he run? Was he so loyal to his family that he would take revenge on Rebecca and her parents? Or did he care more about his own skin? In spite of the heat of the shower, his face still sent a shiver down her spine.

"Put it out of your mind, Rebecca. Put it out of your mind," she kept saying to herself.

Meanwhile, rushing for the front door, bag over her shoulder, Sarah Roberts stopped for a moment to give Jasmine a hug and a kiss.

"Take care, Jaz. Just keep an eye on your sister and brother, hmm? And lock up after I'm gone."

"I will," she replied, giving her Aunt an extra big squeeze.

"BYE REBECCA!" shouted Sarah Roberts up the stairs. "BYE JAMIE! BYE EMILY!" she called through the closed door of the family room. No reply.

No surprise there, she thought. *That TV's loud enough to deafen people living on Mars. Sounds like 'Dr Who' is on. At least the two of them aren't worrying about everything like we are. Lovely to be so young.* She pulled open the front door and slammed it behind her, not registering that it had already been unlocked.

Rebecca strolled into the bedroom, still towelling her hair, while Jasmine began packing her few things into a small bag. Rebecca stopped.

"Oh," she said, disappointed.

"What's up?" Jasmine looked up at her.

"I didn't think…" said Rebecca. "I mean, it hadn't hit me that…"

"That I was going?" Jasmine gave an unsmiling grin.

"Yeah," Rebecca sat on the edge of her bed, watching her cousin. "Anything I can help you with?"

"Nah. Not much to do," said Jasmine.

There was an uncomfortable silence for a minute as Rebecca finished drying her hair and Jasmine completed her work.

"You will keep in touch, right?"

The sentence hung in the air for a moment. Jasmine looked incredulous.

"Course I bloody will! Whadda you think?" Rebecca blushed and gave one of her beautiful smiles.

"You're on Facebook, right? And we can text and email."

"Yeah, yeah. And Instagram and WhatsApp!" Jasmine continued: "We prob'ly won't see each other for six weeks. It's going to be really bad: six weeks of Dad's stupid comments and Mum saying nothing about it. But he's not going to get away with it. I'm not going to shout and yell, but if he says, 'Oh why aren't you nice and skinny like Rebecca?' I'll just say, 'It's the genes, Dad. It's 'cos *you're* so fat!' Then I'll smile and walk away."

"Good for you!" laughed Rebecca – Jasmine had mimicked all Uncle Gary's actions and facial expressions, perfectly. "That'll sort him!" Rebecca wouldn't miss Uncle Gary; but six weeks away from Jasmine? That would be hard. She sighed. "We'll get through the term somehow, Jaz...hey, I've had a brainwave: maybe you can go on holiday with us, somewhere! I'll ask Mum. I'm sure she'll say yes, because she's really pleased we're friends!"

Jasmine's face lit up for a moment, then darkened again.

"Wha' about Jamie and Emily? They'll want to come, too. Unless we can get Mum 'n' Dad to take them somewhere else...Becks?"

"What's up, Jaz?" asked Rebecca.

"I haven't seen Jamie or Em. Are they *still* watching TV?"

"Yeah, must be. TV's on."

"Hmmf!" said Jasmine. "They need to get their stuff packed." She marched to the bedroom door and shouted down the stairs. "Oi! Jamie! Emily! Get upstairs, now!"

No answer.

"Little beggars. I'll sort 'em out." Jasmine stomped downstairs to show them she meant business. Rebecca followed, giggling. Jasmine stormed in to the family room. "It's empty!" She picked up the remote control and turned off the TV. "Are you hiding behind the sofa, again? 'Dr Who' ain't that scary, y'know!"

The girls checked behind the sofa. No children.

"I'll look in the garden while you check upstairs," said Rebecca. She dashed outside while her cousin combed the house. Rebecca searched every bush, tree and hiding place that she could think of, but nothing. She ran back indoors.

"Did you find them?"

"No! D'you think they went outside on to the road?"

"They'd need the key," replied Rebecca. "Mum would never tell them where it was."

"Hah! Em's really sharp when it comes to watching what people do. I'll bet you she found it!"

"Oh no." Rebecca turned pale: she remembered how many of her own things vanished when Emily was around. "Come with me." Rebecca hauled her cousin out to the main door and found the fresh-faced, ginger-haired PC patrolling.

"Hello. Can I help you, girls?" he asked.

"Have you seen my cousins? A girl and a boy aged seven and five, playing out here this morning?" Rebecca queried.

"Not seen *any* kids today," he said, smiling brightly. "Why?" He immediately realised what a stupid question it was. His smile evaporated. "Come with me and we'll have a look together." As he entered the house he sent a message on his mobile informing his office of what he was doing.

For the next fifteen minutes the three of them minutely checked the house, the garden and the integral garage. They looked in all the smallest nooks and crannies they could find and even in the loft, even though they knew the children were too small to get up there.

Again, the young PC spoke rapidly into his mobile to update his office: more help was needed – the children were nowhere on the property and a search of the immediate vicinity outside the property was needed. Within five minutes, the response team were at the door, taking full descriptions of the children from Rebecca and Jasmine.

For the next forty-five minutes, the police went door-to-door, asking if anyone had seen the children that morning. The girls watched, helplessly, by the side of the young PC at their gate – Rebecca, biting her nails, Jasmine, frowning, her right hand compulsively gripping and releasing the flesh on her left arm, leaving temporary, white finger-marks on the pink skin as the hand moved up and down the limb.

Finally, the officers came together to confer with each other. After a few moments, one came towards them. Jasmine held Rebecca's hand, tightly.

"Negative at the moment," he said, gently. "We're going to extend our search to the surrounding roads and we've sent an alert to all the areas nearby, with a description of your brother and sister. That's all we can do for now. We've been to all the houses on your road, except two across the road where there's no answer and now I'm going to go to your next-door-neighbour's house…"

"Wait!" Rebecca shouted more loudly than she intended. Her cheeks reddened in embarrassment and her explanation tumbled out of her mouth faster than Simone Biles performing back handsprings: "That's Ida Dehmobedi's house. I think I should go with you, 'cos she's a friend of mine and she's elderly and she's already upset about Alice Denisov's disappearance, so if you turn up asking about my cousins it'll be a massive shock for her, so please let me go with you!"

The officer looked doubtful at first, but then relented.

"Ok. I'll let you lead. But I *will* need to ask the questions."

Rebecca nodded her thanks.

"Jaz, I know you're worried but it's best if I go in to Ida's without you."

"But…" protested Jasmine; Rebecca gently touched her cousin's cheek and quietened her.

"It'll be too much for her if too many of us go in, 'specially with you so upset, Jaz. It's going to be tough on her…I don't want to make it any worse than it already is."

Jasmine's chin trembled.

"Be quick, all right?" she said hoarsely.

Rebecca nodded again and left Jasmine with the young PC.

Leading the other police officer over to Ida's front door, Rebecca knocked and waited. Thirty seconds later, the door opened. Rebecca found herself staring straight into a man's chest! Looking up, she saw the broad, smiling face of Caleb Samuels.

"Hey, Rebecca! What can I do for you?" he asked, jauntily, dispelling her momentary shock.

"Oh, of course, it's Friday. You do Ida's shopping."

"That's right. Carl and I been having tea and a chat since we got back from the supermarket."

"Excuse me sir, you don't live here?" the young PC came from behind Rebecca.

"Eh? Oh, sorry officer. Didn't notice you there. No, I'm from number 12. I go shopping for Ida… Mrs Dehmobedi, on Fri…"

"Did you say number 12, sir?" asked the PC. Caleb nodded. The PC glanced over at Rebecca. "That's one of the houses where there was no answer. We're going house-to-house asking people if they've seen this young lady's cousins: a seven-year-old and a five-year-old who went missing some time between 7 and 10 am."

Caleb Samuels' face dropped.

"Oh God...not again."

"Who is it, Cal?" Ida's voice called from deep within the house. "Who's at the door?"

He turned his head and called back down the corridor.

"The police are here with Rebecca. Her cousins have gone missing!"

There was silence, then a rapid padding of slippered feet down the corridor. Ida's pale face appeared at the door.

"Oh darlin'! Come in, come in!"

Inside Ida's living room, Carl Jenkins and Caleb Samuels went to get some tea and chocolate biscuits for the police officer and Rebecca.

"Thanks," said the officer, "it's been a long day already."

Ida stroked Rebecca's hand as she spoke:

"Jus' can't believe it. Your Emily and Jamie! Why?"

"We don't know for sure what's happened, yet, Mrs Dehmobedi. All we know is that they're missing. They could've wandered off and got lost..." began the PC.

"But you don't think so, do you?" cut in Carl Jenkins, earnestly.

"Well, it would be a big coincidence," admitted the officer.

"You mean, after the other child?" Rebecca's gaze was firmly on the PC's face. He nodded, then he looked across the room.

"Mr Samuels, Mr Jenkins, did either of you see the children this morning?"

"No. We went out shopping at about, uh, what time was it Cal?"

"Eight o'clock," answered Caleb Samuels, checking his watch. "I didn't see no one on the road, this morning. Very quiet, in fact."

"An' the kiddies never came round here, neither," put in Ida.

"God, it's becoming an epidemic…child kidnapping!" Mr Jenkins banged his fist angrily on the table. Caleb Samuels put a comforting hand on his shoulder.

"Well, we really don't know, yet, Mr Jenkins," said the young PC. "Thanks for your help, all of you and thanks for the tea and biscuits, too," As he got up, Carl Jenkins shook his hand, then Caleb Samuels did the same. "Nice chain, sir," said the PC, noticing the one on his wrist. "Reminds me of something one of my relatives used to wear."

"Thanks. Had it for donkey's years. Brings back great memories." smiled Caleb Samuels. Rebecca ignored it – she was thinking about her cousins.

"See ya later, darlin'." Ida gave Rebecca a firm hug.

"Thanks, Ida," she said, returning the hug.

The officer dropped Rebecca at her house and continued the search. Jasmine was waiting at the door.

"Any news?" her eyes pleading for something positive.

"Nothing," Rebecca replied. Her cousin slumped down on the white porch bench. Rebecca sat next to her and put her arm around her. "Jaz?"

"What?"

"Jaz, I think we'll have to let your family know what's happened."

"Ohhh…" groaned Jasmine.

"*And* Mum."

Jasmine groaned again.

"You know we have to," continued Rebecca. "I'll phone them if you like. But they need to know." Jasmine sank back into the coats, hanging up behind her, but she nodded, slowly.

Moments later, Rebecca was ringing her uncle's mobile phone.

"Typical. It's his voicemail, Jaz!" Rebecca called out.

"Maybe he's driving. He said he was going to pick up Mum from the hospital," answered Jasmine. "I bet he goes back home before he listens to…"

She was interrupted by two loud chimes from the front door bell. Jasmine rushed to open it.

"Look who's all better!!"

Aunt Leanne's arms were wide open. Jasmine flung her arms around her mother and burst into tears. "There, there, love. It hasn't been that long since you saw me! I couldn't wait to see you all!" She grinned and hugged her, tightly. "Where're Ems and Jamie, then? I've got some presents for them. Oh, hello Becks."

"Hi, Aunt Leanne. I've been trying to ring Uncle Gary," said Rebecca, quietly.

"And here I am, Becksy, babe!" came her uncle's jovial voice. "How's about a hug for me!" Rebecca gave him a half-hearted hug. "You can do better than that!" he laughed.

"Not today, I can't," she replied.

"Ahh...what's the matter, Becksy? Have you and Jasmine fallen out again?"

"No...it's much worse." Rebecca led them into the family room. "Emily and Jamie have gone missing!"

As Rebecca and Jasmine explained the events of the last few days, Jasmine's parents grew paler. As one, they sat down with a bump on the sofa. Jasmine's mother spluttered and tried to speak; her father's mouth hung open, but he said nothing. Eventually, Aunt Leanne regained her composure:

"This is your Mum's fault! She goes off leaving two children to look after little ones and now Ems and Jamie have gone missing – maybe kidnapped by some maniac! Why my brother ever married your Mum I'll never know!"

"HOW DARE YOU!" Rebecca roared, her eyes blazing like her scarlet cheeks. "My Mum and Dad have done everything to help you! They're fantastic parents and they love Jaz, Em and Jamie!"

"They've been bloody brilliant while you've been in hospital, Mum," added Jasmine, indignantly. "They've taken care of us like we're their own kids!"

"Don't argue with your Mum!" retorted her father. "If they're such good parents, how come Ems and Jamie are missing? If I'd been here..."

"But you weren't, were you?" shouted Jasmine. "You were watching football on Sky all the time we was here! You thought Mum being in hospital was a holiday for you, didn't you, Dad? 'Time away from the kids?' 'Peace at last', was it? You don't care about us! You *never* cared about *me*! All this is YOUR fault!"

"Don't you go giving lip to your father, young lady!" interrupted her mother. "You've been a bad influence on our Jasmine, Rebecca!" she shouted, wagging her finger in Rebecca's face. "She was never like this before she stayed here. What have you been saying about us behind our ba…"

"Stop it, stop it, STOP IT!" Jasmine was shaking with rage. Aunt Leanne froze: never had she seen Jasmine so angry. "Becks is one of the best friends I've ever had and she was there for me when Alice was…" she broke off for a moment, her chin trembling, "…taken."

Her mother lowered her eyes and bit her lip. "Sorry, sweetheart, I didn't realise…"

"'Sorry' don't cut it no more!" yelled Jasmine and she ran out of the room. A moment later the outside door slammed, loudly.

Aunt Leanne elbowed her husband. "Go after 'er!"

"Wha'? Me?" Uncle Gary shook his head vigorously. "You 'eard 'er: she won't listen to me!"

"I'll go," said Rebecca, without looking at either of them, her cheeks still fiery red. As she headed for the inside porch door, the house-phone rang. She hesitated. Jaz or the phone?

Instinct said Jasmine; head said phone.

She went for the phone.

"Hello? Mum…uh…hi…how's Dad? He's awake! Oh, good, great! Give him my love, Mum. What? Jaz, Jamie and Em? Um…are you sitting down? I–I've got a lot to tell you."

Ten minutes later, Rebecca replaced the phone in its cradle on the little hall table and gathered her thoughts. What next?

Jasmine.

Rushing outside, she ran straight into the young PC.

"Hey! Careful, young lady!" The young police officer managed to keep his feet and stop Rebecca from rebounding into the silver birch by the gate. "What's going on?"

"Sorry. Sorry. I just...did you...did you see Jasmine, my cousin? She ran out about ten or fifteen minutes ago, really upset."

The PC shook his head.

"I heard the door slam when I was patrolling round the other side of the house. By the time I got here, there was no sign of anyone." He immediately spoke into his mobile phone that sat mid-way between his left shoulder and the centre of his chest. He gave Jasmine's description. "I'm sure she'll turn up in no time," he told Rebecca.

Voices and a door closing caught Rebecca's attention. Was it...? No. Not Jasmine. Carl Jenkins and Caleb Samuels saying goodbye to Ida and crossing the road.

"Go back in the house," said the officer. "There's nothing you can do out here. We'll find her." Rebecca nodded, reluctantly and went inside.

In the kitchen, Rebecca found her uncle and aunt making a pot of tea.

"Would you like a cup, Becksy?" Uncle Gary asked her, sheepishly.

"Yes please. Milk and two sugars."

"Here you are, love. Biscuit?" Uncle Gary proffered her favourites with chocolate and caramel toppings.

"No thanks," she replied, miserably.

"Look, love," said her aunt with a Jasmine-style, lop-sided smile, "I'm sorry about what I said about your Mum; I know she cares about our three. And Jasmine'll be back soon, I'm sure. She sometimes gets in a sulk at home and goes off for a bit by herself. But she gets over it quickly."

"I hope you're right," said Rebecca, with unnatural calmness, "'cos it's dangerous out there...*really* dangerous. And if she gets hurt, I'll never forgive you." Her aunt and uncle exchanged an anxious look.

For the next twelve minutes, they sat in silence, drinking tea: Rebecca stared, unblinking out of the window; her aunt examined her bright red, painted nails; her uncle scratched – his head, his nose, his ear and finally his belly.

Then Sarah Roberts arrived.

Her face was red. She was seething.

Her focus was entirely on Rebecca. Like her daughter – twelve minutes earlier – her voice was completely calm and controlled, but ice-cold.

"Why didn't you phone me as soon as you knew the children were gone?"

Rebecca went pale. Why did she always feel guilty when her mum spoke to her with that voice?

"I–I thought that...I mean, I didn't want to...wo–worry you, about...I mean with Dad in ho–hospital... I–I got the police to look..."

"Come on Sarah, she's doing her best..."

Uncle Gary's interjection was cut short by Sarah Roberts' steely-eyed glance. Seeing her clenched fists at her side, he returned to scratching his head.

"He's right!" declared Aunt Leanne. "She's had a lot to deal with. And they're *my* kids! You can't expect a thirteen-year-old to make all the right decisions when there's so much pressure on!"

Sarah Roberts blinked in surprise. Her sister-in-law defending Rebecca? Her fists slowly unclenched, as she let out a long breath.

"Maybe you're right, Leanne," she said, nodding, her eyes fixed on the slate tiles of the kitchen floor. Maybe I was expecting too much. Too much …it's all too much…"

Her hand slowly covered her eyes and her shoulders shook. Aunt Leanne put her arms around her. Rebecca stood transfixed. Uncle Gary sat staring at the scene – embarrassed – scratching his neck.

"I, uh, I'll make you a cuppa tea, Sarah," he said.

Rebecca felt useless. Aunt Leanne was comforting her mother; her father was being treated in hospital; the police were searching for Emily, Jamie and Jasmine; even Uncle Gary was making some tea; but there was nothing for her to do.

Slipping out of the kitchen, through the short corridor and out of the back-garden door, Rebecca wandered across the patio flagstones on to the grass and sat heavily in front of the array of lilac, chrysanthemums, phlox and roses that filled the flower bed.

It was warm and relaxing in the sunshine. A Painted Lady butterfly zigzagged a path past her head and alighted on a large, buddleia bush, so gently, that the pinkish-purple blossom barely moved under its weight. She noticed the orange-brown wings with black and white spots on the forewing when they were open and the mottled brown undersides with spots when they closed. Rebecca watched it take in nectar through the proboscis. So lovely. Just sitting, observing nature in her own garden. How could anything terrible be happening on such a beautiful day?

Suddenly, the butterfly flew off, startled by a passing robin. The bird landed a few metres away from Rebecca, but seemed completely unconcerned by her presence. It hopped bravely past her, with its greenish-brown feathers and orangey-red breast on show. In the nearby flowerbed, it began pecking at the soil with short, quick movements, searching for tiny insects. It remained there for a full minute, finding its prey in abundance. Rebecca gazed at it, contemplating.

"I hope nothing eats you, robin," she said quietly, "I'd hate to think of you as part of the food chain..."

Rebecca immediately jumped up. The robin – scared by the abrupt movement – flew off like a shot. Rebecca fumbled in her back pocket till she found what she was looking for. Staring at it, intently, she tightened her lips into a smile.

In a moment, she was out of the back gate that had kept 'Satan' at bay three nights earlier. Racing across the shingles, she dashed past the PC at the entrance to her home.

"Hey! Where do you think you're going? Come back!" he shouted.

"Follow me!" she yelled back at him. Rebecca heard him mumble something incoherent into his mobile, but she didn't wait. She knew where she was going and she knew what she had to do.

Flinging open the gate of 12, Pine Tree Close, she marched down the path.

BANG-BANG-BANG!

Rebecca hammered on the bronze door knocker with such force, that the entire house seemed to shake.

"What're you doing?" the young PC demanded, puffing behind her.

"Just follow my lead," answered Rebecca without turning round.

No answer came.

She pressed her face up against the frosted glass pane in the door.

"Can't see anything. Can't hear movement…" She clicked her fingers. "Of course! Next door!"

Leaping neatly over the low wall that separated the two properties, Rebecca moved swiftly to the front door of number 11 and rang the doorbell and rattled the knocker.

After half a minute, she heard the sounds of locks clunking and a chain being unhooked. The door opened. Rebecca looked directly into the smiling eyes of the bespectacled face above her.

"Oh, hi Rebecca. I wondered who was knocking so hard."

"Sorry, Mr Jenkins," Rebecca said, innocently. "Can we come in, please?"

Carl Jenkins had a perplexed smile on his face, as his eyes flicked between her and the PC in tow.

"Well," he began.

"It's just for a moment. It's really important." Rebecca smiled her most dazzling smile.

"Well," he said, "I guess so. Come on in. I was just chatting with Caleb in the back garden." Rebecca led the way into the house, followed by a very confused PC and – a couple of seconds later – by an even more mystified Carl Jenkins.

As she entered his house, which was a similar design to Ida's, Rebecca was struck by the differences: the corridor had a light, clean decor. Every surface of the wall and skirting board was in pristine condition, as if it had just been painted. Entering the living room, the pale brown, wood floor, which extended from the hallway, looked perfect. In the middle of the room, a laptop sat open upon a low, solid wood coffee table, that stood upon a soft, pale rug. Two identical, comfortable armchairs sat either side of the rug. Again, the room was spotless: not a speck of dust, not a stain, not a scratch.

To the right of the coffee table stood the fireplace in the same position as Ida's; but, whereas her fireplace was a typical, pinkish, ceramic-tiled rectangle with an ugly base (over which Rebecca had regularly tripped), Mr Jenkins' was a white marble, art deco rectangle, with an inverted chevron motif overlapping the top of the fireplace and stretching down into the rectangular, stepped opening, in which small, carefully chopped logs sat in readiness for the winter months. The base was neat and clean.

Above and either side of the fireplace were several, neat shelves, full of trophies.

"Oh, are you a golfer, Mister Jenkins?" asked the PC, as Rebecca moved to the window, admiring his equally tidy garden, where Caleb Samuels was examining one of the plants. He turned, and, noticing Rebecca, gave a surprised smile and a wave.

"Yes. I've played for the local club for many years," replied Mr Jenkins, beaming.

"What did you win that one for?"

The PC was pointing to a large trophy with a golden golfer in full swing, upon a tall, white plinth, with a bronze plaque. Carl Jenkins handed it down to the officer to look at.

"That was when I was club champion, oh, about fifteen years ago. My handicap was only seven then."

"Hmm. Very impressive, sir," replied the PC, examining the trophy. "My handicap is still thirteen, but I'll keep working at it." He returned it carefully to its owner. Just then the kitchen door, to the side of the right-hand trophy cabinet, opened and Caleb Samuels entered. He came over to stand next to his friend.

"Well, what is it that's so important, then, Rebecca?" asked Carl Jenkins, turning towards the window where she was standing. "How can I help you?"

Rebecca swung round and smiled; but this time her smile was different. All the warmth had vanished.

"I know," she said as she thrust a small square of card up to Caleb Samuels' face, "and here is my proof."

"What?" His brow furrowed as he looked intently at the card. Then the frown deepened as he slowly turned to look at his companion, who was also staring at the card.

The PC looked puzzled and stepped forward to have a look at the card.

"Proof? Proof of what…"

The sentence was never finished. A moment later, he was lying on the floor, unconscious. He never saw the trophy slamming into his left temple. He never saw his attacker standing over him, hyperventilating.

"You killed him! You killed a policeman. What the hell have you done, man? Give me that, before you hurt any…Aghh!" On the floor, next to the young police officer, lay a groaning Caleb Samuels.

Rebecca struggled to understand what had just happened. She was frozen to the spot: all traces of her confident smile had gone. Carl Jenkins turned on her, the trophy still gripped tightly in his hand. He had the mien of a very scared and very dangerous wild animal.

Rebecca backed away to the window, edging to her right. Carl Jenkins advanced on her, brandishing his trophy like some mediaeval mace, angry tears streaming down his face.

"Everything. You've...ruined everything!" He lunged at her, aiming the trophy at her head. She instinctively ducked and went into a shoulder roll, ending up by the armchair furthest from the window; Carl Jenkins' momentum sent him crashing into the wall below the window, the force of the blow shattering his trophy against the wooden floor. He struggled to his feet and turned to face her.

Rebecca kicked the armchair, violently. It skidded across the room and smashed into Carl Jenkins, who crumpled under the impact. She turned and dashed out of the living room, down the short corridor. Reaching the door, she turned the handle and pulled it hard. It opened a few centimetres and stopped, short, jerking the handle out of her hand. It had been chained! With trembling fingers, she struggled to unhook it. When the chain fell away she pulled the door again, and dived through the opening, yelling at the top of her voice:

"Help! HELP!"

Powerful hands grasped her shoulders and yanked her back into the house. With his left arm wrapped around her neck, Carl Jenkins hauled her down the corridor towards the living room. Rebecca – screaming, writhing and feet kicking – dug and raked her nails across his bare forearm, forcing him to bellow in pain. He twisted his body to the right and flung her back into the living room. She fell, headlong, over the two bodies and into the coffee table, which slid into the fireplace, taking the rug with it. Her head caught the corner of the table, sending a lightning bolt of pain through her skull.

Dazed, she tried to focus on her attacker. He was leaning against the doorjamb, panting and examining the damage to his scarred, bleeding arm. His eyes were malice. He started towards her. Rebecca tried to get up, but her heels skidded on the polished floor and she fell against the armchair near the window. Carl Jenkins threw her into the chair and gripped her throat, pushing her slowly up the back of the armchair. His face contorted as he began to squeeze. Fighting, slapping, punching and kicking, Rebecca ripped off his spectacles and scratched his right eye. His right hand left her throat and clutched his face, but his left hand only momentarily relaxed. Then it resumed its pressure: she felt the pain of her throat being slowly crushed. Her body jerked, her eyes bulged, her mouth wide open, her hands trying to prise open the powerful fingers as she struggled for breath.

She knew she was going to die.

"AAAHHH!"

Carl Jenkins lurched backwards, his left hand flying up and away from Rebecca. She wretched as the air rushed back into her lungs through her tortured throat. Rebecca collapsed on to her hands and knees, her eyes shut tight, sucking in huge gulps of air.

A violent struggle was now erupting around her, but she had no strength to lift her head to see it. Ornaments clattered furiously across the floor, a chair was thrown over, glass smashed and heavy feet stumbled in staccato bursts on the wooden floorboards. Two voices were shouting and screaming unintelligibly: one deep and harsh; the other, higher, ferocious. A battle raged, but who? When she finally managed to raise her head, she was astounded.

Carl Jenkins was spinning around, arms flailing, desperately trying to throw his screaming attacker off his back.

Jasmine!

She had locked herself around Carl Jenkins, her arms grasping his neck tightly, her legs gripping his stomach, trying to avoid his attempts to get a hand hold of her head and shoulders. Suddenly, he managed to grasp her hair and began to pull her over his right shoulder. Immediately, Jasmine sank her teeth into his neck and bit as hard and deeply as she could. Carl Jenkins howled in agony and staggered backwards into the wall, knocking the wind out of her. Involuntarily, she released her grip. He struck out, blindly, behind him, his gold wristwatch catching Jasmine across the face. She fell to the floor, holding her bleeding mouth, momentarily stunned.

For a few moments, he crouched in front of Jasmine, his chest heaving. Eventually, he spoke.

"I'll finish you as well," he hissed at her, unsteadily picking up the remains of a heavy trophy from the floor.

"Carl!"

Caleb Samuels' steely fingers gripped Carl Jenkins' arm as he pulled himself up from the floor to his full height. All the while, Carl Jenkins tried to wrench himself free. For what seemed an eternity, the two former friends wrestled for control of the weapon, face-to-face, teeth gritted, sweating and wounded, neither giving an inch. Finally, Caleb, bloody from the gash to his head, ripped the weapon out of Carl Jenkins' hands, before his own legs buckled under him and he fell, exhausted, to the floor. In desperation, Carl Jenkins grasped the golden golf club that hung over the fireplace and swung it backward, two-handed, intent on recommencing his attack on Jasmine.

Leaping up next to the coffee table, grabbing the nearest object, Rebecca screamed:

"Jenkins! NO!"

Carl Jenkins whirled round baring his teeth.

The laptop smashed into his disfigured face.

He dropped like a dead deer.

"Jaz?" Rebecca let go of the laptop, flew across the room to her cousin and flung her arms around her. They were both shaking and breathless, but after a minute Jasmine said:

"I'm…all right. I'm all right! *You* call for the police and ambulance and I'll tie '*im* up!"

While Rebecca made the call, Jasmine found a couple of large tea towels in the kitchen. She rolled them, length ways and tied Carl Jenkins' hands, tightly, behind his back and then did the same to his feet. Rebecca began applying a pack of frozen peas to the swelling on the young PC's head, while Jasmine very gently wiped the blood away from the large cut on the left side of Caleb Samuels' forehead. Then she found some ice, which she put in a clean cloth and applied it to the wounded area to reduce the swelling; neither she nor Jasmine could bring themselves to administer any aid to Carl Jenkins.

Within a few minutes, four squad cars appeared on Pine Tree Close, rapidly followed by three ambulances. The paramedics took over from the girls and tended to all the injuries. Attention was then given to Jasmine's bleeding mouth.

"No broken teeth, then," grinned the tanned, young medic. "Looks like you get to keep that perfect smile." Jasmine beamed at him. Rebecca, who was having her throat checked by another, older medic, raised her eyebrows, knowingly at her and mouthed 'perfect smile' at her. Jasmine winked back.

"Your throat is going to be sore for a week or so," said Rebecca's medic, "judging by the bruising. But no serious damage."

Sergeant Smith, meanwhile, supervised the removal of the wounded men to the ambulance, ordering his officers to keep a host of onlookers from the neighbourhood back behind a perimeter. He directed PC Sharma and a PCSO to stay with Carl Jenkins, whom she promptly handcuffed to a stretcher rail. The injured young PC was taken away in a separate ambulance, followed by one of the squad cars stationed outside the house.

Caleb Samuels, however, remained seated at the kitchen table with Rebecca and Jasmine, refusing to leave, despite a medic's encouragement.

"I ain't goin' to hospital till I get some answers! What the hell just happened?"

"I agree, Mr Samuels," said Sergeant Smith, returning from the ambulance. "Young lady, tell me in detail what made you come over here with one of my officers and how and *why* this…this…incident occurred?"

"Yeah," said Jasmine, "I'd like to know why we jus' put that madman in 'ospital…apart from, like, he was trying to kill you…and me!"

Rebecca raised a brief smile at Jasmine's comment.

"Well, when you were out on a strop…" she began.

"Oi!" shouted Jasmine in mock horror. Rebecca winked at her and continued.

"…I remembered something I'd seen." She pulled out the small piece of card from her jeans and showed it to each of them in turn.

"Why are we looking at this, exactly?" asked Sergeant Smith.

"That's a picture of that girl, Catherine Rayburne, who disappeared thirty-five years ago!" exclaimed Jasmine.

"What? The girl disappeared?" Caleb Samuels sounded incredulous.

"That's right," said Rebecca, "but can you see what caught my eye in the picture?" she said to the Sergeant.

"Hmm. She looks a lot like you, actually, Rebecca." Seeing Rebecca shaking her head, Sergeant Smith resumed his inspection of the photograph. "No distinguishing marks of any kind. She's wearing a gold chain around her ne…" Sergeant Smith stopped. "Hold on," he said, thoughtfully, "it's…" he turned slowly to his right and both Jasmine and Rebecca followed his gaze.

"Yeah, it's the same one I'm wearing on my wrist. I recognised it when you showed us the photograph earlier on," said Caleb Samuels. "But today is the first time I've seen that girl, I swear!"

"Then how come *you're* wearin' it!" shouted Jasmine. "How'd you get hold of it?"

"Okay, okay, young lady, before you start makin' accusations you'll regret, let me tell you a story, about myself, so you know what sort of person I am and how I ended up with this chain.

"I came to England from Trinidad back in 1975, thinking I could make a better life for myself. So I went to college. Life was hard for a young, black man, then. It ain't easy now, mind. But back then I had a tough time finding a place to live and a job. Lotta prejudice to deal with from a lotta people.

"Well, I put myself through college, by doin' evening jobs and working weekends till I got my accountancy degree. Finally, I got myself work in a bank in Tottenham. I worked damn hard and finally, after ten years of working my way up, I got promoted to manager." He grinned at the memory. "The first black manager *ever* in that bank. Put a few noses out of joint, I can tell you!

"During that time I met Marian, the love of my life, at our local church. We got married and then in 1990, I transferred down here to another bank and moved in next door.

"I met Carl shortly after we arrived. He was all alone – his mum had died some years earlier – so Marian and I took him under our wing. We got on like a house on fire: we both played golf and he knew all the golf courses around here. Pretty soon we became best mates. We were a real family, the three of us.

"But Marian was hit by cancer in '96…she…she passed away two years later. That was hard. So hard." He broke off to wipe his eyes for a moment. "But I was lucky, because Carl was always there, supportin' me. I couldn't have asked… for a better friend."

"What's all this got to do with Katie's necklace that you're wearing, now?" demanded Jasmine.

"I'm comin' to that, young lady. Well, on my fiftieth birthday, back in 2001, I had a big party with family and friends. I got given a load of expensive presents, but y'know, it was Carl who gave me a really special one: this gold wrist chain. He knew I liked real gold, so it meant a lot when he gave it to me. It even had...had a 'C' for *Caleb*!" He continued to speak, fighting back tears. "When you came over, Rebecca, and showed me the photograph, I recognised the chain... I was just about to point it out to Carl... when all hell broke loose."

"So, Catherine disappeared while you were still living in Tottenham, Mr Samuels," continued Sergeant Smith.

"Then when I showed you the photo," said Rebecca, "Mr Jenkins realised you'd say that it was a present from him. That's why he attacked your officer, Sergeant."

"Of course," said Sergeant Smith, "he knew he was about to be found out."

"I've seen the chain on you many times since I was a little girl, Mr Samuels," said Rebecca, "but it was only this morning that it hit me. I should've realised yesterday when I was given Catherine's photo, or Katie, as Mr Rayburne always called her. Just can't work out why I didn't connect the two, yesterday?"

"You had a lot on your mind, Rebecca: your Dad in hospital, worrying about your family and friends," said Sergeant Smith, kindly.

"But why did Mr Jenkins keep it? An' why did he give it away as a present? Didn't he know he could get caught?" Jasmine asked.

"Trophy," said Sergeant Smith. "Some criminals keep things that belonged to their victims as a trophy of the crime. It gives them a twisted feeling of superiority over the police, dangling a clue in front of their noses and some sort of personal connection to the victim. But giving something that important away to another person who had no connection with the crime? *That's* unusual. Mr Samuels?" A red-eyed Caleb Samuels looked up, giving the officer his undivided attention. "I think that, however sick Carl Jenkins is – and he is very sick – I think that his giving you the necklace as a wrist chain for your birthday...well, maybe it was his warped way of showing that he really *did* care for you as a friend."

Caleb Samuels sighed, deeply and removed the chain.

"That's as maybe, Sergeant; but I can't keep this chain any more. It belonged to that poor girl and now to her family. And I guess it must be evidence or something like that?"

"Something like that," the officer replied and allowed him to drop the chain into the evidence bag.

"Besides," Caleb Samuels continued, "what man in his right mind would want to keep a gift from a kidnapper and a murderer?"

"I understand," replied Sergeant Smith. "Look, we really need to get you to the hospital now, Mr Samuels. You can give us a formal statement, later."

"Sounds good to me," replied Caleb Samuels, getting up unsteadily and taking the arm of a supporting medic.

"Mr Samuels," said Jasmine. "I didn't say it before, 'cos I had to know about the chain."

"What d'you want to say, young lady?"

"Thanks. You saved my neck just now." And she hugged him.

"My pleasure, young lady," he replied, with a gentle smile. "You take care."

Rebecca and Jasmine watched as Caleb Samuels was helped into the final ambulance and driven away.

"Don't worry Becks," said Jasmine, "He'll be fine."

"Yeah, You're right. Hey! I never asked you!" exclaimed Rebecca.

"What are going on about, now, Becks?"

"Where'd you come from just now, Jaz? After you left the house we thought *you* might've been kidnapped!"

"Nah! I went for a walk to cool off, I was that angry with Mum and Dad. I was coming back to your place but there wasn't a policeman by the gate, so I looked for him. Couldn't find him. Then I heard you screaming. I followed the yelling and found the front door open. So..."

"...you ran in and saved my life!" said Rebecca, gratefully.

"Yeah...true...but you saved mine, too," replied Jasmine, the pain in her mouth stopping her from grinning too broadly. "God, you really hit 'im, Becks!"

"Well, he was trying to kill my cousin...my friend," replied Rebecca. Jasmine blushed, then nudged Rebecca hard in the ribs.

"Oi! I know why you didn't work it out, earlier, about the chain!"

"Why?" queried Rebecca.

"You're so slow, Becks! One, 'cos you always thought of her as 'Katie' instead of 'Catherine' – K instead of C? Two, 'cos it was a *neck* chain on Katie and a *wrist* chain on Mr Samuels! Think about it: he's got big wrists – about as big as a young girl's neck, yeah? But you did guess...sort of. Not your fault it was a gift from the killer!"

Rebecca looked down in embarrassment and nodded.

"Yeah, you're right, Jaz! You'd make a good detective."

"Whatever," replied Jasmine, looking suddenly depressed. "If I'm so good, why can't I find Em and Jamie?"

"Don't beat yourself up about it, Jaz: you saved my life. He would've killed me. We've got to leave it up to the police to find…" Rebecca paused. "Jaz? What's up?"

"Becks," said Jasmine, "why is there a bigger gap between the floorboards there than anywhere else in the room?" She pointed towards the section of the floor that had been uncovered when the rug had been dragged across the room, during the struggle with Carl Jenkins.

"Sergeant Smith? What do you think?" asked Rebecca.

The officer crossed the room, removed the coffee table and threw back the rug.

"What have we got here?" he said. "Looks like a trapdoor to a basement."

"But the houses here don't *have* basements!" exclaimed Rebecca.

"This one does," he replied, pulling up on a recessed, stainless steel door-ring. With great physical effort, he dragged up the trapdoor. Its wooden top covered 7cm of concrete. Resting the open trapdoor against the coffee table, the officer shone his flashlight into the opening. A set of steep, perfectly cuboid, concrete steps led down into the darkness. Crouching just above the top step, he craned his neck to either side and squinted into the basement.

"I'm going in," he said simply. The two girls rushed to his side. "Not a chance! You two wait over there. I don't know what's down there, but it's my job to find out, not yours!" Jasmine was about to argue but the resolute expression on his face made her think better of it. "Simmons! With me."

"Yes Sarge," replied a very slim, red-haired PCSO.

Sergeant Smith began his slow descent, down the steep steps, still in his crouched position, torch beam flashing its powerful light ahead of him, followed closely by the PCSO. As they disappeared into the basement, Rebecca felt Jasmine's hand gripping her arm. Her own hand closed over Jasmine's as they listened to the sounds of the two officers moving around beneath them.

An instant later, an exclamation came from the basement, along with scraping and muffled whining. More back and forward voices. What was happening? Rebecca inwardly screamed for an answer.

As if in reply, footsteps – heavier ones this time – began ascending the steps. Jasmine, hardly breathing, tightened her grip on Rebecca's arm, making her cousin wince. Gradually, figures emerged from the basement; but whereas two people entered the basement, *four* came out.

The officers were carrying two small, dirty, shivering shapes, tear-stained and frightened.

"Emily! Jamie!" Jasmine dashed forward and hugged her brother, then her sister, as well as the officers holding them. "You're ok! You're ok!" She kissed them both, again and again; eventually, Sergeant Smith had to call a halt:

"Enough, Jasmine! That's three times you've kissed me! Good thing you're not wearing lipstick or my

missus would be asking me some difficult questions!"
He grinned and glanced over at the blushing PCSO who
was still being kissed almost as much as her little
brother. "Ok, leave young Simmons alone: his cheeks
have turned the same colour as his hair! Right, let's call
for the medics to check out your brother and sister." As
he said this, PCSO Simmons got on to his mobile to call
for immediate medical assistance for the two children.

"But they're all right aren't they? He didn't hurt
them, did he?" asked a worried Rebecca.

"As far as I can tell they're fine, yes, but it's procedure
to get victims of serious crime, like kidnapping,
medically checked. They'll need to go to the hospital for
a thorough examination."

Jasmine nodded and stepped back to give the officers
some space. For the first time, she noticed the red, raw
marks around the children's wrists and the anguish in
their eyes. Angry tears began to fill her own, but she
fought them back. She wasn't about to do anything to
scare her Jamie or Emily. She turned her back, quickly.

"I hate Jenkins *so* much, Becks!" she whispered,
hoarsely. "I wanna…"

"I know, I know," replied Rebecca, "I feel the same.
But we got him. He's not going to do that to anyone
else."

"Your parents are going to come with us to the
hospital where we'll get Emily and Jamie checked out,
Jasmine," said Sergeant Smith. "Rebecca, your Mum is
waiting for you at your house. I'll brief PC Shah on the
details of what's happened and send him with you to
explain exactly what's been going on. Don't look so
worried."

Rebecca gave a brief, half-smile.

"Thanks, but you don't know my Mum!"

"So...tell me again why I shouldn't ground you for a month?"

The question hung in the air for several seconds. Sarah Roberts glanced over at her daughter for a moment to see if she had been listening, then refocused on the road ahead. Rebecca's eyes remained firmly fastened on the line of traffic in front of them. "Well?" her mother persisted. Rebecca had hoped to avoid this conversation. She thought it would be okay after PC Shah had spoken with her Mum and they had both followed her Uncle, Aunt and cousins to the hospital. The doctors had said that the children should stay in, overnight. They would arrange for them to talk to a counsellor trained in dealing with children who had been through traumatic experiences. Rebecca and Jasmine were amazed when Uncle Gary said he'd stay there, overnight, to be with them. After giving Jasmine a hug and her own Dad a big, goodnight kiss, Rebecca and Sarah Roberts had headed for home. She finally answered her mother.

"Well...I did solve the case of that missing girl, Katie... Catherine...from thirty-five years ago. Mr Jenkins would never have attacked the officer if he hadn't known that he'd been found out. I mean, Sergeant Smith said that they'll probably find her body under the basement fl..."

Rebecca suddenly realised what she was saying.

"Yes, Rebecca," said her mother, "they'll probably find her body under the basement floor. Catherine was a real person, you know, not just a story character. Just think about that. You met her parents; she went to the same junior school that you did; she had her own friends; Ida and Shahin loved her…just as Ida loves you, now; but Catherine was kidnapped and she was murdered. Her life was snuffed out – taken from her when she was younger than you are, by a man who has no conscience, no feeling, Rebecca. A man who pretended to be a kind, caring member of the community for all these decades and…"

"…and that could have been me."

"Yes – it could have been you." Sarah Roberts gripped the steering wheel so tightly that her knuckles turned white.

"Sorry." The word barely left Rebecca's throat, it was so tight. But her Mum's hand reached across and squeezed hers.

SATURDAY

The sun streamed in, again, through the deep pink curtains into Rebecca's eyes. This time she threw back the duvet, dived into the shower and was soon downstairs making breakfast for her Mum, who arrived a few minutes later.

It was strangely quiet in the house. No Jamie or Emily scurrying about, laughing and screaming, making a mess, or running off with things that didn't belong to them. No Jasmine sitting on the other side of the kitchen table, giggling while they chatted. No telephone ringing...

"BRRIINNNGG, BRRIINNNGG!"

Rebecca and Sarah Roberts looked at each other. They had the same thought. Terry Roberts. They both grabbed for the phone; Mum got there first.

"Hello? Yes? Speaking. Oh, hello. Yes? That's confirmed, now is it? Yes, I thought so. It is very sad, isn't it. I suppose you'll have spoken to...Mmmm. I'm sure that wasn't easy. Have you found...You did? And? That's great news! So what was it all ab..? Uh-huh. Really? No, I'd have th..."

Rebecca was listening, avidly and with increasing irritation. Who was she talking to? What was it about? The one-sided conversation continued for some time.

"Right. Ok. Well that explains it. Yes, we will. No, we haven't changed our minds. What about...? Yes... you read my mind. Mmhmm. What has he said? What... everything? Really? Wow! Makes things much simpler, then."

Rebecca was furiously miming 'Who is it?' faces at her mother, who waved her away. Grabbing the phone off her mother was fast becoming an attractive option. Sarah Roberts continued her conversation, oblivious to her daughter's visual histrionics.

"Right. Yes, that's fine. Thank you so much for the call. Bye now." Sarah Roberts put the phone down and looked at her daughter.

"Well?" Rebecca was exasperated. Sarah Roberts burst out laughing. "Mum? Stop it! Tell me who that was! Come on!"

Sarah Roberts was doubled over, now, her laughter erupting like the thunderous waters of Niagara. "Mum...Mum...GROW UP, WILL YOU!"

After another half minute the laughter subsided. Sarah Roberts wiped the tears from her eyes and looked up at her daughter. Rebecca was eyeing her with pursed lips, slitted eyes and folded arms.

"Feeling better, now, are we?" Rebecca asked, icily, doing an excellent impression of her mother.

"Oh yes. Yes. It was good to laugh. You should have seen your face...it was just like me! Ha–ha–ha! OK, OK!" Sarah Roberts continued, still smirking. Then she became more serious. "That was Sergeant Smith. He phoned to update us about a few things.

"Firstly – sadly – they positively identified Catherine's body in the cellar." Rebecca's hand flew to her mouth. "Her clothing matched the descriptions in their records from the time of her disappearance, the size of the body matches and the dental records clinched it. They've already informed her parents, of course. Poor parents. Thirty-five years of not knowing..." she sighed deeply.

"Why the hell were you laughing, then?" asked Rebecca, aghast.

Sarah Roberts looked embarrassed. "I wasn't laughing at that, honestly. It's just that, I've been wound up tighter than a coiled spring for so long and then this call...well...the relief, and then...and then...the look on your face..."

Sarah Roberts creased up laughing all over again, slapping the table-top hard as she laughed. Rebecca rolled her eyes to the ceiling and waited, tapping her foot, impatiently.

When her mother had finally got herself under control, Rebecca said: "Relieved about what?"

"Well, Sergeant Smith also updated me on the men that attacked your Dad. Apparently, that... THUG..." she spat out the word, "who got away when the police raided the house opposite? They caught him. Seems he has nothing to do with kidnapping children!" Rebecca's eyebrows shot up in surprise.

"But those noises in the garage..."

Sarah Roberts shook her head.

"What you heard were animals. Rare animals that are on the endangered species list. He confessed everything to the police, hoping for a shorter sentence when it goes to court. They import the animals illegally from poachers in the country the animals come from. Then they sell them on to unscrupulous buyers. They can make a fortune that way. They thought you'd worked that out and sent the police to check it out. That's the reason they wanted to intimidate us." Her daughter began shaking her head. "Rebecca, what's wrong?"

"It just doesn't make any sense, Mum. We *know* Carl Jenkins kidnapped Catherine. The police didn't find any other children in his basement. So, if it wasn't him, *or* the men who broke in here, then *who* kidnapped Alice Denisov on Sunday night?"

Sarah Roberts shrugged her shoulders.

"I guess that's for the police to find out, *Detective* Roberts."

"Yeah," replied Rebecca giving an unsmiling grin. "Hey. What time is it? Oh, it's nearly ten! I'd better hurry."

"What's the rush, Rebecca?"

"Gotta see Ida!"

Dashing outside, slamming the door behind her, Rebecca raced across to her neighbour's house. She couldn't wait to see the delight on Ida's face when she heard the good news – those lovely crinkles and creases round her eyes and maybe even a few tears of joy.

"No milk on the doorstep," said Rebeccca to herself. "Must be making tea. Good timing! I love her tea!" She knocked firmly on the door. It moved. Rebecca pushed it open as she knocked again. "Hello? Ida? Your door is open. Are you in the kitchen?" She entered the familiar, dark corridor, closed the door, tightly and walked towards the living room from which the TV news channel was blaring. "You didn't shut it properly," she said, passing through the half open living room door, "when you brought in your milk."

An open carton of milk lay on its side, the white liquid dripping on to a growing, pale stain on the brightly patterned carpet. One of Ida's precious, porcelain cats lay in pieces on the nearby fireplace. Rebecca suddenly felt very cold, inside.

"Ida? Where are you? Ida! Where are yo..." Something was in the shadows. Something small, lying between the tea trolley and Ida's favourite chair. She rushed over to a small form. Breathing rapid, shallow breaths, Ida's face looked grey and pained.

In seconds, Rebecca had put Ida into the recovery position she'd learned in school, called 999, gently placed a thin cushion under her head and a small blanket over her body to keep her warm as she waited for the ambulance.

Hours later, Rebecca and Sarah Roberts sat in the reception area of the Intensive Care Unit. Doctors and nurses had been in and out of the unit in what seemed like perpetual motion. Sarah Roberts cradled her daughter's head in her lap, silently stroking her hair. She hated hospitals and she hated waiting for news, even more; yet here she was, again. What was happening to her world?

The door to the unit abruptly opened and a tall, tanned woman, with wavy, brown hair tied back into a tight bun and wearing a white coat, entered reception. Looking around, she spoke:

"Is there a Rebecca Roberts here?"

"Yes!" Rebecca jumped up.

"My name is Dr Janeke." She spoke in a clear, clipped, South African accent. Her hazel eyes made contact with Rebecca's green ones. "I have been treating Mrs Ida Dehmobedi."

"Is she okay? Can she go home soon?"

Dr Janeke broke eye contact with her.

"No, Rebecca. She's very weak. Is this your mother?" Rebecca nodded. "Hello Mrs Roberts," she said, shaking her hand. The doctor looked from Sarah Roberts and then back to Rebecca. Her lips narrowed and she scratched her left cheek with a delicately boned finger. The cold feeling returned to Rebecca's bones. Rebecca squeezed her mother's hand, tightly. "Her prognosis is not very good. Her heart is weak. I'm very sorry," said Dr Janeke. "But she's been asking for you, Rebecca."

"Come with me, Mum, please." Sarah Roberts nodded and they quietly passed through the doors and along the bright, antiseptic corridor. Passing each doorway, Rebecca could see elderly patients with pale-faces and sunken cheeks, eyes firmly closed. One was breathing deep, harsh breaths, each one a struggle.

Reaching the last door, Rebecca was relieved to see that Ida had regained some of her colour, but she looked weak and tired. As they approached her bed, her eyes flickered open and she smiled one of her gentle, crinkly smiles.

"'Ello love."

"Hi, Ida," said Rebecca, taking one of her hands and lightly clasping it.

"Thanks for finding me, darling."

"What happened?" asked Rebecca.

"I was making tea for two – I knew you'd come round – and I was listening to the news on the TV. That was when they said that they'd arrested a man for kidnapping two children and on suspicion of murdering a girl many years ago…and…and it was Carl Jenkins! When I 'eard that, everything went black…and then I woke up here." She stared hard at Rebecca. "It's true, isn't it? He kidnapped your cousins and killed little Catherine?" Rebecca nodded. "And I never guessed. He was in my home, Becca, smiling, laughing, bringing me shopping…for the best part of forty years!" Ida gripped Rebecca's hand with unexpected strength, her eyes ablaze. "D'you think he helped me 'cos he felt guilty about Shahin taking the blame? Or 'cos he was laughing at me!"

"I don't know." Rebecca's throat was tight and she could hardly see through her misty eyes. "But we got him, Ida. We got him and now everyone's going to know that Shahin was innocent. I'm going to make sure that all those newspapers that wrote those awful things about him, eat their words! I promise."

Ida rested her head back on her pillow.

"Thanks, darlin'. But there's something else I need you to do. Maybe even more important."

More important? Rebecca was surprised, but she answered: "Sure, Ida. Anything."

"Come closer, love. Let me whisper it to you."

Rebecca leant in as Ida whispered, her furrowed brow gradually relaxing as Ida finished. Rebecca sat up and nodded. Ida smiled, weakly, her eyes slowly opening and half-closing in a gentle rhythm, as if she was very sleepy. She lay, silently, for several minutes as Rebecca and Sarah Roberts watched over her. The room and the rest of the unit outside the room became quiet. Rebecca watched her breathing: it was smooth and regular, not like the other patient she'd seen.

"Becca? Are you still there?"

"Yes, Ida."

Ida's eyes were only half open now, but there was an intensity in them.

"You do know, Becca…I'm not worried. I'm not worried at all."

"Not worried about what, Ida?"

"About never going home again."

Rebecca was shocked.

"What do you mean? Of course you're going home!"

"No, love," she smiled, "not any more. Going to see Shahin." Her hand lifted, unsteadily, towards Rebecca's cheek. She stroked it. "Never had my own children, darlin', but I'd have been proud to have you as my daughter."

Rebecca held Ida's hand tightly against the wet tracks on her cheek.

THE FOLLOWING SATURDAY

At 4.15pm, a solitary figure wandered down a wide, tree-lined cul-de-sac with a large, grassy area, some 50 metres from the main road, where many young children still chased each other happily around its ash trees and threw balls to each other.

"126...128...130...132...134 Ash Road."

Pushing open the wooden gate with the crumbling blue paint, Rebecca retraced her steps up the small red and white diamond-shaped tiles where the grass grew even longer through the gaps. Passing the grimy, cracked, whitewashed walls and the blistering paint on the window frames, she reached the doorway and knocked firmly on the door's pebbled glass pane, three times. Rebecca found herself counting the pebbles in the glass, while she waited. Then she became aware of a fragmented shape becoming larger and more coherent through the glass. A face peered through the window at her for a few seconds. The door opened.

"Oh...it's you!" said Mr Rayburne, surprised. "The police gave us the news about Katie, you know. Thank you for finding her." Then he looked her up and down, noticing the dark trousers, shirt and jacket. "You're dressed very smartly. Important occasion, no doubt." He seemed embarrassed. "Well, uh, you'd better come in." He called ahead to the living room: "Julie! We have a visitor."

Mr Rayburne led her into the room, which was still stuck in its time warp. There, Mrs Rayburne sat, a small tumbler of amber liquid in her right hand, dark shadows under her eyes. She looked up and groaned.

"Ugh! It's you! Come to gloat have you, child?"

"Julie! Don't speak like that!" exclaimed David Rayburne.

"Why? It's true, isn't it? The newspapers are full of what you and your friend did – true heroines, the pair of you!" Sarcasm dripped from her voice. "So they've caught the real killer. So I was wrong about who took my daughter. So I made a mistake. Come for an apology, then, have you?" she said, in slow, bleary blinks. "Wasn't the one in the papers enough?"

"It was on page six, Julie," said David Rayburne, "and it was a very small acknowledgement that they'd got it wrong."

Julie Rayburne got up, unsteadily, from her chair and staggered over to stare directly into Rebecca's eyes. "Well, you're not going to get an apology from me! Not even a small one. I had a right to be angry...and it's not my fault that man died."

"Shahin, Julie," said Mr Rayburne, quietly. "*That man* was called *Shahin*."

"So what?" Mrs Rayburne glared at her husband, before turning back to Rebecca, breathing waves of whisky fumes into her face. "You tell Ida, from me...she lost her *husband*...but I lost *my daughter*! She was part of me," she said, her fist hitting her chest. "I carried her for nine months and raised her for nine years! She was my life!"

"No," said Rebecca.

"No, what?"

"No, I won't tell her, Mrs Rayburne," said Rebecca, calmly.

Julie Rayburne's eyes narrowed as her lip curled upwards.

"You're an arrogant girl, aren't you?"

"No, Mrs Rayburne," replied Rebecca, "I'm not arrogant. I won't be telling her, because I've just come from Ida Dehmobedi's funeral." Julie Rayburne's sneer faded. Rebecca continued: "I can't imagine what you must have felt all these years, Mrs Rayburne. I can't imagine what it would be like to have my only child taken from me. I can't imagine the feelings that made you lash out at Ida and Shahin. But both of them were good people and didn't deserve your hate. They really loved Catherine. They really loved you and your husband, too. And they really loved each other.

"So, I won't be delivering your message to Ida, Mrs Rayburne. But I am here to deliver a message *from* her."

"What?" She looked over at her husband and then back at Rebecca. For the first time, Julie Rayburne actually looked frightened. "Wha–what did she say?"

Rebecca paused for a moment, took a deep breath and said:

"I forgive you."

The whisky glass fell from Julie Rayburne's hand, bounced and emptied its contents on the olive-green carpet. Her face crumpled. Her shaking hand covered her mouth and silent sobs wracked her body. David Rayburne rushed over and she collapsed against him. They held on to each other in the middle of the room, as if no one else in the world existed: her arms tightly wrapped around his back; his arms cradling her; his face nestling into her hair.

Rebecca slipped noiselessly from the room and left the house.

That night, Rebecca lay on her bed, gazing at the ceiling. A myriad of thoughts entered and exited her mind, some floating through, gently, for her to pick apart; others flying in and out in a flash with barely a moment to grasp them. A theme seemed to emerge from her daydream. A universe of change had occurred in her life – there seemed little resemblance between her life two, short weeks ago, and what it was now. Ida, Jasmine, Dad, Katie, Alice, life, violence, death, revenge, forgiveness...they all spun round in her head.

Her thoughts were interrupted by her phone. Jasmine!

"Hi Jaz. What's up?"

"Becks! You're not gonna believe this!"

"What, Jaz?"

"She's alive! She's alive!"

"What? Who? Slow down! I can't understand what you're saying!"

"Alice! She's not dead! Alice is alive!"

"But–but...how? Why? I mean...that's fantastic!" Rebecca was amazed but full of questions. "What happened, Jaz? Did she get lost or something?"

A loud peal of laughter roared out of the phone. Rebecca held it at arm's length. Eventually, Jasmine eased down to a soft chuckle.

"No, dingbat! I got a call from her Mum. Alice rang her from Russia and..."

"RUSSIA?"

"Yeah, Russia! Alice's Mum and Dad split up six months ago and it was a bad breakup. Mr Denisov left home and he hadn't been back to the house in all that time. Alice used to visit him at his flat every other weekend. Well, he kidnapped her and…"

"Alice's Dad *kidnapped* her?"

"Yeah, well…not exactly *kidnapped*…"

"Then *what* exactly, Jaz?"

"Shu' up and let me finish, willya? Anyway, her Dad picked her up off the street. He had her passport and he had some of her clothes from when she stayed with him at weekends. He told her that her Mum had agreed to it, so she never argued with him. He took her straight to the airport and off to Russia. An' that's where she is now."

"Why didn't he tell Mrs Denisov after he took Alice? She must've been out of her mind, worrying."

"Like I said: it was a *bad* break-up," said Jasmine.

"How's she feel about being over there?" asked Rebecca.

"She said it was ok at first – seeing all her Russian family was great. But now she's missing everyone here. I reckon she wants to come back."

"So, when *is* she coming back, Jaz?"

"Dunno," sighed Jasmine. "Could be months… could be years!"

"Why?"

"Depends on if Alice's Mum and Dad can sort things in a friendly way. If it gets legal, it'll be a long time, 'cos Russian law is different from ours. Hey! Maybe we should tell her Mum about that agency that brings back kids from other countries!"

"Yeah," laughed Rebecca, "at least our research would have been useful to somebody. I'm sorry, though, Jaz. I know Alice is important to you. I really hope they can work it out."

"Thanks, Becks. But...I s'pose I'm lucky. My parents can be pains," said Jasmine, "but they love each other and I guess I love 'em too."

"True."

"How *you* feeling, Becks?"

There was a long pause.

"I miss seeing Ida every day," Rebecca answered. "I could always turn to her for advice. Wish you'd got to know her better, Jaz. You'd have really liked each other."

"Yeah? Why's that?"

"'Cos you both speak your mind!" Rebecca heard a chuckle from the other end of the line. "You'd have loved her tea, too. She was special."

"Yeah. Must've been."

"Hey, my Dad's coming out of hospital tomorrow! Doctors say he's going to be fine. No permanent damage."

"That's great," said Jasmine through a barely stifled yawn.

"Sorr-ee if my good news is keeping you *awake*, Jas-mine!"

"No chance of that, Becks!" Rebecca could hear her grinning.

"How're Em and Jamie doing, Jaz?"

"They're a lot quieter," replied Jasmine. "Nervous of strangers, too. Mum says they'll get more counselling to help them. It's gonna be a while before they get back to normal."

"Yeah, you're probably right," replied Rebecca.

"Ohh, yeah…Nearly forgot," said Jasmine. "Got a surprise for you."

"Another one?" Rebecca frowned. "Nothing could top that one about Alice!"

"Yeah, well, it's a different sort of surprise. I dropped in this afternoon to see you, but you was out. I didn't come alone, either. I'm gonna love 'n' leave you now. Just check in the box next to your bed. G'night, Becks."

"Good night, Jaz," Rebecca said, baffled by Jasmine's cryptic comments.

Looking over to her left, she saw the small, brown, wooden box with inlaid mother-of-pearl her Dad had made for her when she was a little girl. It had a concealed hinge and always opened noiselessly. She had kept special things in it when she was younger, but now it was just a keepsake of her Dad.

She picked up the box and carefully opened it. A piece of partially folded paper popped up. Rebecca gently unfolded it. On it were two, small, smiley faces with yellow hair drawn in coloured pencil. Two words were written, neatly, in blue, capital letters:

'THANK YOU'.

Rebecca frowned again.

She peered into the box.

Then…

…she smiled.

She understood.

Her world really *had* changed.

Out of the box, Rebecca removed her silver ring with little red and green stones set in circular patterns.